CONTENDERS

▼

CONTENDERS

STORIES BY
TERENCE WINCH

Story Line Press

ISBN: 0-934257-23-X

Book design and cover painting, *Knockout,*
by Susan Campbell

Acknowledgments:
The Washington Review, Carousel Review, Fiction 84, Fiction.
The author also wishes to thank Patrick J. Clancy for his help
and the D.C. Commission on the Arts and Humanities for a grant that
assisted in the completion of this book.

Published by Story Press, Inc.
d.b.a. Story Line Press
403 Continental Street
Santa Cruz, California 95060

for Kevin, Pat, and Eileen

to Cathy
good to see
you in Columbia
Thanks.
Terry Winch
11 Feb 94

CONTENTS

▼

SMARTASS

McCARTHY AND I were drinking beer in O'Grady's bar in West Farms. O'Grady said something to McCarthy about settling down, finding a nice girl. McCarthy scoffed at this advice. He was in his mid-twenties at the time, out of the Navy after four years, and working as an insurance man. He thought he was doing all right. He said something clever to O'Grady like "fuck you," but he leaned over to me with a confidential air and embellished his response.

"I just want to fuck around, make some money, have a good time," he told me.

"I can understand that," I said.

"Last thing I wanna do is get married," McCarthy said.

"You're too fat to get married," I said. I was a wise guy.

I didn't see him for about two weeks after that. Which was unusual, since we spent a lot of time together in those days.

Then he came into O'Grady's one night and told me he had met this girl and was engaged. Once again he was very confidential. Not a word to anybody. McCarthy sometimes acts as though the Thought Police are hot on his trail.

"She's great," he told me. "Incredibly beautiful. Very independent."

"Sounds good," I said.

He dropped out of sight again and there were rumors about family intrigue, opposition to the marriage, that kind of thing. I respected him. McCarthy is always finding new and complicated ways to exercise his talent for never knowing what he is doing.

Tommy Keenan called me up one Saturday morning at ten a.m.

"McCarthy asked me to call you," Keenan said. "He's getting married at noon and wants you to be there."

"How come he didn't call me himself?" I asked. I was insulted. I get insulted very easily, though I'll never admit it.

"Well, he's really busy with the arrangements and shit," Keenan answered.

"Yeah, right," I said.

My father had given me a cheap but pretty mandolin. There was a party downtown after McCarthy's wedding and I was asked to bring my mandolin. The party had no connection with McCarthy's marriage, except that a few of us who were at the wedding also wound up at that party.

One of the people in our entourage was Big Tom Kennedy. Kennedy was enormous and very strong. For a long time I had considered Kennedy to be a big goon and nothing more. He was ten or fifteen years older than me and very intimidating. He was gruff to children. When we were kids we always stayed out of Tom Kennedy's way.

But McCarthy started hanging around with Kennedy. They went on long binges together and became friends. "Kennedy is no dummy, he just looks dumb," McCarthy told me. "He's actually a pretty smart guy. He's good protection too."

It was hard to overcome my lifelong impression of Kennedy as a big simpleton with a mean streak, but I started seeing him more from McCarthy's point of view and my opinion of him changed. Once McCarthy even brought Kennedy with him to my apartment while they were on a binge. I didn't know what to expect. I thought maybe Kennedy would tear the furniture apart and eat the cat. But he was a complete gentleman in his own way and I could see why McCarthy liked him.

Kennedy was, however, very conspicuous at this party we went to after McCarthy's wedding. The party was thrown by a hip couple who lived in a nice apartment in a bad neighborhood, which was itself a hip thing to do in those days. Without McCarthy, who was presumably enjoying his first night of connubial bliss, Kennedy was at a loss. There was no way for him to fit in. This situation seemed to depress him and expand his legendary appetite for alcohol.

The rest of us were getting very drunk too. Besides Kennedy and me, there were three others in our group: my brother Jesse, Willie Farrell, and Tommy Keenan, the guy who called me that morning about McCarthy's wedding. Jesse and I played for a while at the party. I played the mandolin my father had given me. It didn't have a case. I would have to get one to protect it from the elements.

I'm very paranoid and didn't like the idea of getting back home from the neighborhood we were in. It was not a comfortable place to be in, especially if you were white. I'd rather be safe than hip. But at least I wasn't alone. Not only was I not alone, but I had in my company the fearsome Tom Kennedy. In fact, all five of us were reasonably big men. So I figured everything would be all right. We'd catch a cab, head for West Farms, and maybe have a few beers in O'Grady's.

We left the party. As soon as we hit the street, Tommy Keenan dropped a bottle of Drambuie we had with us. It was in a paper bag. We looked into the bag, hoping against hope that the bottle hadn't broken in spite of the fact that we heard the glass shatter when Keenan dropped the bag. When people are drunk they value alcohol more than when they're sober. The loss of the Drambuie made us sad.

We headed for Amsterdam Avenue to catch a cab. I carried my naked mandolin by the neck, but I was so drunk and paranoid that I almost forgot I had it with me. Big Tom Kennedy was very quiet, perhaps still feeling the sting of not fitting in at the party. But who knew what thoughts lurked inside his gigantic head? Certainly not me.

There are times when you want a cab so bad, when just the sight of the bright yellow car with its "taxi" light on driving out of nowhere to rescue you causes great joy and relief. No cab appeared. We continued staggering along. I was not drunk enough to be unafraid. But Big Tom Kennedy was right out there in the street, flagging down imaginary taxis. There seemed to be nobody around but us.

No one, until a group of about forty black people turned a corner and appeared on the other sidewalk. They were heading in the opposite direction. They looked like they might be coming from a dance or something. I said to myself, it's all right, everybody looks happy. I tried to communicate silently with them to let them know that sure, we're white, but once you get to know us we're real nice, and we're sorry to be on your turf, folks. Really.

And everything was cool, they were going their way and we were going ours, until Tom Kennedy—massive, drunk and confused—stepped out into the middle of the street and did the unthinkable.

He began to taunt the crowd.

He stood in the middle of the street and yelled "Oh Yeah!" at the crowd, trying to mimic a black comedian who used that expression in his routine. Maybe it was the late Godfrey Cambridge. I don't remember. Over and over he boomed out "Oh Yeah!" at the black people.

Oh God, Jesus, please, Kennedy, No! Stop! I thought to myself. The four of us stood on the sidewalk in stunned disbelief. Kennedy was throwing us into very hot water. This is the end, I thought. These people will cross the street and destroy us.

But nothing happened.

I felt so good, so thankful, that we were spared. It had a hypnotic effect on me. Kennedy remained in the street baiting the caravan of black people as they disappeared down the block. What decent people, I thought. The rest of us stayed on the sidewalk and watched him. We had geared up for disaster and nothing happened. Now it would take a minute to shift back to normal.

Then something happened.

I saw these three young black guys heading for Kennedy. They must have been with the crowd of dancers. It was hard to figure out why they were coming back. I mean, unless they had guns and were planning to shoot us, there was no real reason for us to be scared. And it didn't seem like they would shoot us when they could save that particular risk for more worthy targets. If they didn't have guns, then they were the ones taking the chance by so foolishly coming within the range of Tom Kennedy. Kennedy alone could probably put these three away before they knew what hit them. But Kennedy wasn't alone—the four of us were there to back him up if he needed it.

It was Kennedy who never knew what hit him. They were so fast that Kennedy seemed to be going down, sinking to his knees, before they even got to him. Jesus Christ, I thought, what are these guys—from Outer Space? Mighty Tom Kennedy had fallen. He wasn't getting up for a while either.

Then I saw Willie rolling down the street. That's what it looked like. As though he were a human wheel. Holy shit,

I thought, these guys mean business.

Big Tom and Willie were down. Me and Tommy Keenan and my brother Jesse were still on the sidewalk. We were stunned. The booze was wearing off. It was clear to us that these three black dudes could take all of us with absolutely no sweat. What the fuck was it? Magic, Karate, something. I didn't know.

My mind struggled through the effects of alcohol and fear to think of some way out of this. Then I knew what I would do. I would simply explain to these guys what the story was: Kennedy, the big one, was drunk and didn't know what he was doing and the rest of us were definitely not looking for trouble. Maybe they were nice guys, gentlemen. Yeah!

I stepped off the curb, about to deliver my little speech.

One of the black men looked at me and said, "Get back on the sidewalk with your fucking banjo."

It wasn't a banjo, but that mandolin again. I had forgotten it was still in my hand. I didn't argue and got back on the sidewalk.

The next day I had no idea what happened to the mandolin. It was nowhere to be found. I remembered that I took a cab home with Willie and met the other three guys in O'Grady's. They had taken a cab ahead of us. I was real scared waiting there with Willie for a cab, but I figured the worst was over.

Those three black guys turned out to be all right. After they told me to get back on the sidewalk, they abruptly walked away. Jesse and Keenan and me had escaped what we thought was our inevitable fate. Big Tom and Willie weren't hurt too bad. I guess those black men just wanted to teach us a lesson.

It wasn't until weeks later that I thought of Bickford's. Bickford's was a chain of all-night cafeterias. There was one in West Farms. When O'Grady's closed at four a.m. that

morning, the five of us went to Bickford's for breakfast.
The next day I blanked. I couldn't remember what we did
after we left O'Grady's. But now, weeks later, it came back
to me: Bickford's.

I rushed down to West Farms right away. The manager
of Bickford's listened to me. "Oh yeah, a mandolin," he
said. "Yeah, we hold stuff for two weeks. If nobody claims
it, that's it. Somebody took it home," he said.

That mandolin never turned up again. McCarthy stayed
married. He now lives in Yonkers. That's the city where the
Son of Sam was captured. I saw McCarthy last month and
told him that when I first heard the news that a suspect in
the Sam case was picked up in Yonkers, I was worried.
This was before they had an i.d. on the suspect.

"I thought maybe you were the Son of Sam," I said to
McCarthy. I was joking. The worst thing I ever saw
McCarthy do was try to take my hat away from me. This was
at my brother Jesse's wedding party. We were very drunk.

"Don't joke," McCarthy said. "I was coming home
from the Vanguard at about five a.m. one morning this
summer when a cop stopped the cab at a light. He aimed
the flashlight at my face and asked a lot of questions."

"You're kidding," I said.

"I'm not kidding. That police sketch that was all over
the papers looked just like me."

"Amazing," I said.

"The cab driver was impressed," McCarthy said. "He
was this old black dude. When the cop finally split, the
cabbie cracked up. He thought it was great to have a Son of
Sam suspect in his cab."

McCarthy is a little on the heavy side. He loves it when I
joke about his weight.

"But Son of Sam was a lot thinner than you," I said to him.

"Kiss my ass," McCarthy said.

▼

FIDELITY

THE BABY'S DUE in five weeks, my first. I'm not nervous.
We've gone to birthing classes and read all the right books.
I have a midwife named Maggie who I think is fabulous.
Bill, my husband, has been very understanding and sup-
portive. When I'm cranky, he tries to lull me back into a
good mood. Before the pregnancy, we fought all the time.
Maggie has given me lots of great advice. She told me to
tell people the baby is due two weeks after the real date, so
that I won't have a multitude of anxious friends and rela-
tives pestering me. I am hoping for a boy. Bill wants a girl.
He says boys are a lot more trouble.

When I got to the Metro, a middle-aged man gave me a
seat, one of those seats that I think are reserved for the
handicapped. I'm glad chivalry isn't dead. It's tough for
me to stay on my feet for long. People keep telling me how
great I look. I have that special glow common to pregnant
women. I was supposedly beautiful before I was pregnant,
so I guess I'm overwhelming now. What most men don't
realize, though, is that pregnancy is physically more

9

demanding than any of their sports—basketball, baseball, even boxing. That's true. The birth itself is just about the most strenuous experience a human body can undergo.

I don't see Dave much any more, but when I do, it's always a little awkward. He usually tries to kiss me on the lips when we greet each other, and I have to maneuver fast to make sure he kisses my cheek. I took the Metro to Dupont Circle and met him at a Chinese restaurant on 19th Street, and the first thing he did was try to kiss me on the lips. I'm married now. I want plenty of distance between me and Dave.

I tell him that pregnancy is more strenuous than sports.

"Keep dreaming," he says. I protest.

"It's true. Men have no idea how demanding pregnancy is."

"Okay," Dave says, "after you have the kid, we'll play about an hour of basketball and see what you think then."

"I'm not talking just strength," I say. "It's endurance. I'll play an hour of basketball if you'll strap thirty or forty pounds to your belly for a couple of months."

"Hey, I've strapped on an extra twenty already." He pats the little beer belly that has begun to swell noticeably since the days when we were together.

He still looks good, despite the belly. He's thirty-two, has spent five years at his government job, something to do with city planning, and is pulling in thirty-six thousand a year. His camel's hair coat and gold watch must be worth an easy thousand on their own.

"I like money," he tells me. "I'll admit it. I don't like to part with it. I pay my way, no question about it. But I don't throw the stuff away."

God, it's such a beautiful day. Mid-March, the air is clear, the sun shining. A delicate mixture of winter and spring. I don't really want to be here. I'm too pregnant. I feel like a float. Bill jokes that soon we'll need a crane to lift me in and out of bed. I'd like to be home on our screened-in porch, reading a book or listening to music on the headphones and counting the joggers trotting along our street. Our house is already too small and when the baby arrives, we'll really be cramped. But I love it. It's very cosy. It's also the first time I've had a house of my own, after a lifetime of cheap apartments. It's also the first time I've lived in the suburbs. I was terrified of leaving the city. I thought I needed the vitality and energy. But now I don't know if I could go back. My new addiction is tranquility. Peace.

I don't understand why so many men sprout beer bellies right after they turn thirty. Can't they drink one less beer a day or do a few more situps? But then, as everybody knows, it's okay for men to let themselves go. Men are still attractive when they're fifty. Women have to be no more than thirty-five and look like they spend every waking moment at the health spa or beauty parlor. If not, they're over the hill.

Still, I think Dave looks cute. I don't know why he confesses to being cheap. Does he think I'll be impressed with his frugality? Of course, I already know that he's tight with a dollar.

I know a lot of things about him. We met when I was twenty and working as a waitress at a Greek restaurant downtown. He was twenty-three back then, fresh out of grad school and working with two other ex-students as a housepainter-repairman. I liked him immediately. He had a way of jumping up slightly in his chair when he was excited about something. And he would scratch his head in a thoughtful, shy way when he was being very serious or very sweet.

We didn't start going out right away. I had a boyfriend at the time. His name was Noel Myles and we lived together for a year. It alarms me that I can scarcely remember anything about my days with Noel. He worked in a bookstore and we used to visit Dumbarton Oaks when the weather was nice. I'm forever grateful to Noel for introducing me to Dumbarton Oaks. I still go there whenever I can and stroll through the serene gardens whose loveliness continues to enchant me.

But what he was like, or what he and I together were like, I don't recall. I'm terrible at remembering my past feelings. We fought, we made love, we ate out maybe once or twice a month. I remember I would steal baklava from the Greek restaurant where I worked. Noel had a sweet tooth and his eyes would light up when I'd get back from work with a little package of baklava, wrapped in tinfoil, for him. But what we talked about I don't know. I have the vague sense that we were passionate lovers, at least at first. But I have no details of anything etched into my memory.

Dave wouldn't give up, in spite of Noel. He kept calling me up and asking me out and I kept turning him down. Even when Noel answered the phone, Dave would politely ask to speak to me. I was impressed with Dave's gall, and flattered. But Noel got more and more jealous. He started chewing Dave out and hanging up on him. Noel may have been the offended party, but I still didn't like the idea of him hanging up on someone calling to talk to me. My attitude, of course, made Noel even more jealous.

Other people's jealousy is boring. When people define themselves as victims, they seem to invite further victimization. I guess I'm a hypocrite because when I've been jealous, I expect the world to take note and be sympathetic. But Noel's jealousy simply alienated me from him. If he had acted indifferent to Dave's pursuit of me, I'd probably still be with him today. But he got more and more possessive and I backed off. An old story. The more he needed me, the less I wanted him. "You don't own me," I told him, and I started going out with Dave to prove my point. I left the apartment I shared with Noel, moved in with a girl from work, and never saw him again.

Soon after, I installed myself in an apartment with Dave. That was nine years ago. We were together for four years. I quit waitressing right after I moved in with Dave and got a job in Customer Service with Pepco, answering calls all day from angry citizens complaining that their meters had been misread. Dave gave up housepainting at the same time and began his climb up the bureaucratic ladder.

Maggie, my midwife, tells me to watch my weight, but I'm starving. When the waiter appears, I order hot and sour soup, egg rolls, and beef with spring onion. I desperately want a drink and a cigarette while waiting for the food to arrive, but try to content myself with a club soda ....u lime. I have given up everything for this baby. No coffee, tobacco, or alcohol. I had a cold last month and didn't take a single pill. Dave orders another beer and the lunch special, chicken wth peanuts, spicy hot.

"Okay, Dave, why are we here? What's the story?" He had called me yesterday and insisted that we get together. He said he had to talk to me in person.

"Nothing special," Dave says. "I don't want us to lose touch. You're still important to me. I will confess that I just had to see what you look like pregnant."

"So, what's the verdict?"

"Beautiful," he says. "Better than ever."

I haven't seen him for almost a year and have talked to him only a couple of times since then. I told Bill, my husband, that I was having lunch with Dave today. I don't want to be sneaky about this. There's nothing between me and Dave. We're friendly, we keep in touch sporadically, but that's it. I walked out on him five years ago and I didn't look back.

Maybe I'm not great at remembering my feelings, but I do remember vividly how I felt when I discovered that Dave had an on and off "involvement" with a pretty little nineteen-year-old named Marsha, the girlfriend of one of his former partners in the housepainting trade. I was angry. We had a giant fight. He told me it was nothing and it would never happen again. He said he would marry me, do anything I wanted if I would stay with him. The entire experience made me realize how straight I really am. I expect fidelity. I told him I hoped he had a good life and I was out of that apartment that evening and once again crashing with a girl from work.

"I ran into Noel Myles a couple of weeks ago," Dave says. "He said to say hello to you. He lives in Providence now and was in town to see his mother. His mother and father just got divorced after thirty-three years."

"I didn't think you and Noel were on speaking terms," I say.

"Water under the bridge."

To tell the truth, I can barely remember what Noel looks like. I don't even have a picture of him. All I remember are the final months with him, his jealousy and frustration, and my physical desire to get away from him as fast as possible. The food arrives, and Dave and I are silent as we begin to eat. This get-together is triggering so many memories for me. But I feel so distant from it all. The reality of a baby inside you overwhelms the reality of everything outside you. Even Bill says I've been remote. But it's like your interior life has been doubled and the world out there seems diminished.

Dave eats too fast. Chew your food, don't inhale it, I used to tell him when we were together. Men eat too fast. Neither of us talks while we eat, and I find myself going almost as fast as Dave. I love Chinese food. I don't look forward to the trek back home. My legs and feet are starting to ache. Maggie tells me to keep my feet up as much as possible. The waiter returns and clears the table. Dave orders a coffee, I get another club soda.

"Dave, you look good. Prosperous."

"Thanks. I like the job. I almost feel guilty admitting that. So many people I know hate their jobs. I thrive on mine."

"I wish I had learned a profession or taken some computer courses or something. All I ever did was wait tables and work for Pepco. I guess it's too late now."

"Hey, never. After the kid, you could go to medical school or become an astronaut or something."

"Right. Become the first woman President maybe?"

"Maybe," he says. "You're smart, beautiful. Still young. Sexy."

"Don't get forward, Dave. I'm a wife now. Almost a mother." We both smile at each other.

My thoughts wander. Tomorrow I want to get my driver's license renewed. Bill says I should have my license in case of an emergency when he's not around. It's been so long since I've driven that I have begun to think of myself as someone who can't drive.

"Are you seeing anyone these days?" I ask him.

"Playing the field a little," he says. He scratches his head with that shy gesture and I feel a little rush of the old affection for him. Sometimes we seem so programmed. Push the right button, you get the right response.

"Life in the fast lane, huh?" I tease him.

"I've slowed down a bit," he says, "I was drinking too much. And I'm terrified of catching some disease. It's like a mine field out there."

"We talk like we're from different countries."

"I guess we sort of are," he says. He is playing with the empty sugar envelope, rolling it up like a little cigarette, then unrolling it again. Neither of us says anything. I think most of what goes on between people is intangible. I feel myself letting my guard down slightly.

Then Dave says in a whisper, "I still love you." His voice

sounds so sad to me that I'm momentarily taken aback. For a split second my heart plays a trick on me and I feel like Dave and I are back together again. Sometimes I guess our emotions have their own life and chronology, and can leap through time. But I quickly collect myself. I remind myself who I am now, what my life is all about. And I wind up feeling mostly annoyed and impatient with Dave.

"Dave, please, it's a long time ago," I say.

"Don't worry," he says. "I don't have any illusions. I'm a realist. But what I just told you is true anyway."

I am not ready for this. I don't want declarations of love from old boyfriends. Part of me is a little impressed, I confess, that Dave would stray so far from the rules of polite, lunch conversation with a married, pregnant woman. But mainly I feel uncomfortable. I wish the waiter would appear with the check. I am hoping Dave will just shut up. But he doesn't.

"Remember when they did those tests on me, a month or so after you moved out?" he asks. I do remember it. He spent a day in the hospital. His doctor was worried about Dave's kidneys, I think because Dave once had a kidney stone attack.

"Yeah, so?" I say.

"I've never gone through anything so painful in my life. I won't even tell you about it. You don't want to know. The last tests they did, they had to put me out for. General anesthetic. I've always been scared of that. It's like limbo. You're not dead, but you're not alive either."

I can't stand to talk about hospitals, doctors, and sickness. I considered having the baby at home, but Bill and Maggie said no. It's too risky.

"You were supposed to come and take me home. But you never showed up," he says.

"C'mon, Dave. We've been through this before. I'm sorry I didn't make it, I really am, but I just couldn't get there. And I didn't think it was that big a deal."

"You know, when I woke up in the recovery room I didn't know where I was or who I was. It was very unsettling. Then after a few minutes, I started to come to my senses. I didn't have much pain, but I felt very strange and wobbly."

"Dave, we've re-hashed this all before. It's a long time ago. I can't believe you set this lunch up to rake me over the coals."

"I'm sorry. I don't really want to give you a hard time. It's just that I felt a lot of hurt and you never really let me get it off my chest. You used to do that, you know. When you didn't want to hear something, you would somehow cut me off, not let it get out."

"Listen, I'm sorry. I am. It was negligent of me. But we had already broken up and I didn't think it was that big a deal. It wasn't like they operated on you. It was just tests. And I would have been there, but I got stuck at my dance class and there was a thunderstorm. I told you all this long ago."

Most of the time, the baby is very quiet inside me. He, or she, is not the type to do a lot of kicking. Sometimes friends want to put their hands on my belly to feel the baby move, but he doesn't oblige. Now I can tell he is picking up on the strain between me and Dave. I can feel him stirring inside me.

"I took a cab home, after staggering all the way to the hospital entrance," Dave says. "God, I felt like I was on another planet. When I got home, I crawled into bed and waited for you to call. I was so lonely in those days, I guess I just wanted to feel that somebody cared about me."

"Dave, people go through a lot of things worse than those tests of yours. What can I say? I'm sorry I wasn't there. I felt terrible about it. But I don't need you laying a lot of guilt on me. I've got my own up-to-the-minute problems."

"You're right," he says. "I'm sorry. I know I shouldn't be

dredging all this stuff up again. I was stuck on you, though, and couldn't believe it when you left. I thought we'd last forever."

"That's not all my fault, either. Maybe you should have watched your step more," I say.

"I know. I know. You were within your rights. Lately I've been going through some changes and I guess I find myself thinking about us more and more. The way it might have been. It's unfair for me to lay all this on you. I haven't been myself these days. My mother's dying."

"All our mothers are dying, Dave. We're at that age."

"Look, I really am sorry for this. I don't know what I was thinking, and with you pregnant and all."

"Let's just forget it, okay?"

"Fine with me." I just want to be gone. I feel uneasy, weighed down. The baby's restlessness makes me even more impatient. Finally, the waiter appears and silently puts the check on the table.

"I've got to go," I say.

"This is on me," he says, taking out his credit card.

"I'm shocked. You're picking up the whole tab?" I'm just trying to make a little joke to lighten the mood, but Dave looks wounded. Or maybe he's looked that way all through lunch and I didn't notice.

"Are you happy?" he asks.

"Yes. Very," I tell him.

"And the pregnancy's going well?"

"No problems. But it's a burden."

"Well, I hope it all comes off without a hitch."

"Thanks," I say. I shake his hand. He doesn't try to kiss me.

Rush hour has already begun and I wind up standing from Dupont Circle to Metro Center. Maybe chivalry is dead after all. Then half the car empties out before it fills up again. I get a seat. I never stare at people, but I find myself looking at the reflections of the other passengers in my window. I can't wait to get home and relax, be by myself.

After Union Station, the train rushes out of the tunnel and into the daylight, and I feel my shoulders drop with a sigh. The baby quiets down. I worry about Dave. I hope he gets himself together. But right now I don't want to think about him. I try to think of my body when it's back to normal. I imagine me and Bill and the baby at the beach this summer. I want to empty out. I picture myself floating on the water. I tell Bill I want to lie in the sun. Just lie there, my mind blank, nothing but the sound of the ocean, and the day blue and radiant. I can live with that.

▼

CONTENDERS

SHE LIVED WITH a group of people in a beautiful old house on the edge of an affluent neighborhood. The first time he visited her, he was soaked through from the rain. A sloppy, unpoetic rain. She was the only one home. They sat by the bay window, facing each other, and talked. She wore a long skirt and, as always, looked stunning.

"You get a lot of groupies, I bet. The rewards of the business," she said. He laughed.

"No," he said.

"C'mon, tell the truth."

"Very very rarely a woman comes on to you. And it's never the right woman."

"Never?"

"Almost," he said.

She didn't like men. They followed her home from work. They tried to pick her up everywhere. They hassled her on the street. She told him, just before they broke up for good, that she went to a party and some guy kept trying to make time with her and she got so mad she started screaming at him, telling the guy she was not a piece of meat and he should get lost. She laughed and said the guy was shocked at her outburst and she felt sorry for him.

He was jealous when she told him about the guy at the party. She was always telling him about men and their interest in her and how the whole business made her crazy and angry.

But he was different, she said. She liked men who were "in touch with their feminine side." She said she decided to sleep with him when he told her it was okay with him if they never went to bed together. He said he'd be satisfied with just being her friend.

That wasn't exactly a lie. Somewhere inside him he believed it. And somewhere else inside him he knew that's what he had to say to sleep with her. Which was in fact something he wanted to do.

She stood him up on their first date. She said later she was there and made him say, finally, that he believed her. He said he believed her and he did. But he also didn't believe her.

He sat in the restaurant for an hour. He was even ten minutes early. He watched every person who came through the door. He didn't go to the bathroom. He didn't even go to the cigarette machine.

But she never came through that door. She said she came in, looked around quickly, didn't see him, and waited for him outside. Then finally she gave up and left, thinking he had stood *her* up.

He was furious. He was leaving that afternoon for a few days in New York. He thought it would be great to have this first date before he left with this woman who had him infatuated.

His friends in New York asked him how the date went.

"It didn't happen," he said.

*

Once he was in the living room and she was in the
bathroom. She let out a terrifying scream and he ran into
the bedroom. The bathroom was off the bedroom. She was
sitting on the bed crying.

"What's wrong?" he asked. "What happened?" He
thought maybe there was a rat or something. She seemed to
be in a state of shock.

"I turned the light off before I opened the bathroom
door," she said, "but the door stuck. I couldn't get it open.
Then I felt someone grab my wrist. It was so real. Something really grabbed me."

"Well, take it easy. It's okay now," he said.

"You don't believe me," she said.

"No. I believe you."

"You think I'm crazy," she said.

"I believe you. Really." He believed her. He was superstitious. Maybe something did grab her. Some people
swear they've seen statues of the Virgin Mary cry. There's
an American flag on the moon. Anything's possible, he
thought. But he did think she was a little crazy.

She called him when he got back from New York and
said she had been at the restaurant and was sorry they
missed each other. So they made another date.

He got there early again, to the same restaurant, but this
time he waited in front of the place after checking out
everybody inside.

She showed up a little late and looked resplendent. She
was a woman of intelligence and depth. She ate hardly
anything. She ordered a sandwich but didn't eat the bread
and ate only about half of what was between the bread. He
thought that was curious. She was a big and healthy-
looking woman.

*

When he went to her house that first time, he asked her where everybody was. She said they had all gone off on a trip. They started kissing in the living room, by the bay window. Then she said, "Let's go upstairs."

They went up to a big bedroom with a very large bed covered with a thick quilt.

"Is this your room?" he asked.

"No, but I thought it would be more comfortable than mine," she said. She was involved with some guy who lived in the house. He didn't know that till a long time later. When he found out, he figured she must have taken them to the other man's room that day, which seemed like a heartless and disloyal thing to do. But it wasn't the other man's room, she told him when he eventually asked. It housed one of the other women.

They lay on the quilt and fooled around. When matters became more serious, she said, "Let's go up to my room, okay?"

They got undressed. When he took off his pants, she said, "pretty fancy underwear." He had a pair of green Jockey shorts on. He looked at her naked and thought she looked perfect, almost too much so. He told her she was beautiful.

He said to her later, "You're really solid."

"I know, like a truck, right? Very solid."

"You've been told that before, I guess," he said.

"God, all the time."

They were having an argument on the phone and he said to her, "You're terrified of your own vulnerability."

She reacted as though he had discovered her darkest secret and began crying. That was it, she said. She couldn't accept her vulnerability and be open to others. She wanted freedom and independence.

*

He was very much like her father, she told him. He had exactly the same sense of humor as her father. For a long stretch, after almost everything he'd say, she'd say. "That's unbelievable. That's just what my father always used to say." Or he'd do just what her father would do. He got tired of hearing it, so she stopped telling him. But he developed a fondness for her father, whom he'd never met.

She went home to New England for a few days and he called her every day. He thought that would prove how much he cared. She loved getting the calls. She liked attention. "It feels so strange talking to you from this place," she said to him.

He said, "How's it going? You having a good time?"

"It's okay. My parents want me to get a real job, get married. Make something of my life. Anything."

"Did you tell them about me?" he asked. He like attention too.

"My grandmother always asks me about my new beaux."

"What did you tell her?"

"Oh, I told her I met this exciting young man and she would like him," she said.

"That's nice," he said. He felt he didn't rank high enough yet for her parents to hear about him.

"What are you wearing?" she asked.

"Army pants. Red flannel shirt."

"I bet you look real sexy," she said.

"I miss you," he said. "What are *you* wearing?"

"I'm in my room. Naked."

"I wish I was there."

"I wish you were too," she said. "I'm horny."

"No old hometown boyfriends around?" he asked.

She laughed.

*

Months later she went home again. He took her to the train station. They were not getting along. Neither of them had slept much the night before.

They ate breakfast in the station. The woman in the cafeteria said they had to have sausages with their eggs. You couldn't get just eggs. So they got eggs and sausages. He ate his sausages, but she wouldn't touch hers. He ate one of her sausages and they dumped the rest.

"Don't you know what they put in those things?" she asked.

She disapproved of smoking too. But once, after they went to see "Julia," she was so captivated by Jane Fonda as the chain-smoking Lillian Hellman that she grubbed cigarettes from him all night.

"Why do you smoke? It's ridiculous," she said one time.

"Doctor's orders," he said.

He picked her up at the station when she got back. He was there early.

"It's good to see you," she said.

"Good to see you," he said. But he knew she did not think it was that good to see him or to be back in town. He took her bag, feeling like a redcap. She was formal with him. But it was subtle. On the surface, she acted glad to see him.

When they got off the Metro and headed for his place, she began an attack on city life.

"God, I hate this," she said. "It's so noisy and dirty."

"Just life, death, and the human comedy unfolding," he said.

"I'm serious," she said. "I've had it. This is my last year in this town."

"Great," he said. He was hurt.

"Don't pay any attention to me," she reassured him.

"I'm just ranting. I wasn't thinking of you and me. Sometimes I just can't stand the city."

One day in November they had lunch together and he asked her what she was doing the next night.

"I'm busy," she said. She told him she'd be busy the night after that too.

"What's happening?" he asked.

"There's these parties I want to go to."

"Both nights?" he asked. She said yes. He was angry because these were his only two free nights that week.

"Why don't you skip one of the parties?" he suggested.

"No. I want to go," she said.

"I don't understand," he said. "You want to go to two parties on my only two free nights—how do you think that makes me feel?"

"It's not my fault you're working on those nights," she said.

"But if you had only two free nights and I wasn't working, I'd want to see you. The old Double Standard rearing its ugly head again."

She got angry. She didn't like to be questioned. He was angry too.

"Look, if it's such a big deal, I'll skip the party tomorrow night. But it's very important to me to go to the second party."

"What's so important about it?" he asked.

"Look, it's nothing romantic. It doesn't involve sex or anyone else."

"Then why can't you tell me why it's so important?"

"I can't tell you. It's no threat to you. I have to go because of something that's important to me, but it's very embarrassing. Personally embarrassing."

"You tell me you have to go to this party, that it's not because of someone else, that it's deeply embarrassing for you to talk about, and I'm supposed to just accept that. What if I fed you a line like that?" he said. "We're not strangers, you know. We're supposed to trust each other."

She abruptly decided not to go to either party and he had trouble understanding that too.

"Listen," he said, "if it's so important to you that it's too embarrassing to even tell me, maybe you better go."

"No, I don't want to go now anymore," she said.

He met her friend Cathy at the gallery where the two women worked. She told him afterwards that Cathy thought he was very sexy.

"That's good," he said. "She's not bad herself."

"I'll have to keep you two away from each other," she said.

"Worried?"

"Are you kidding? If these women knew how good you are in bed they'd be all over you. Most men are terrible."

"So what do you do, tell all your friends I'm a lousy lover?"

"Listen, that's no joke. I sure don't go around telling them I never had it so good. I never have, either. Had it so good."

One night, right after they met, he was bragging about how great the two of them were and he said to her, "We deserve each other." She laughed.

"I'll remember that," she said. "Better watch yourself, though. It could turn out to be true."

When they were first getting to know each other, he called her "one of life's heavyweights." He said he would take her very seriously if she did the same for him.

Another time, he said to her, "you sorely have my heart beguiled."

"You amaze me," she said. "You say all the right things, even when you're kidding around."

"I'm not kidding around."

28

*

The first movie they went to see was "Looking for Mr. Goodbar." They hardly knew each other. He felt stupid, taking her to see a movie in which all the men are either crazy, impotent, authoritarian, or violent. And all the women, represented by Diane Keaton, are victims.

When they were leaving the theater, they overheard some man in the crowd say to a friend, "Imagine if this was your first date with someone."

They laughed and the tension of the movie was dispelled.

He called her "a beautiful girl" one time and she got insulted. "That's what my father always does," she said. "He's got all these middle-aged women working for him and he calls them 'girls.' It drives me crazy. I'm not a girl. I'm a woman."

"I wasn't using 'girl' as a put-down or a denial of your . . . ." He couldn't think of a word. "Look, I'm your lover," he said. "I know you're a woman. I respect you. But I can also see the kid in you, the girl. Lovers are allowed to do that. I can imagine you as a girl and see that in you. I can imagine you as an old lady too. You'll be a great old woman."

"You sure know how to talk," she said.

"Gimme a break," he said.

"Okay, you can call me 'girl' sometimes."

"Thanks. What a relief," he said.

"Don't retaliate," she said. "You always have to retaliate."

"I'm not retaliating. I'm just reacting to you. Anyway, retaliation implies there's something to retaliate about," he said.

"Let's not argue," she said.

"I'm not arguing," he said.

"You'll be a great old man," she told him.

"Merry-hearted boys make the best of old men," he said.

*

She was in a drawing workshop with her friend Cathy and a few other artists, including Cathy's boyfriend Martin. They all posed nude for each other once a week. She told him how important the sessions were to her. He was not comfortable with the idea of her parading around naked in front of Martin and the others. "This is part of my work," she said. "It's very important to me. Believe me, there's nothing sexual about it."

She went to a party one night. It was another one of those parties he wasn't invited to. The next day she told him that she got really drunk and could hardly remember what happened.

"God, I was a mess," she said. "Martin and Paul Jordan had to bring me up to my apartment and put me to bed I was so out of it." Paul Jordan was a middle-class black he knew slightly from the neighborhood. He wasn't aware she even knew Jordan, but he wasn't surprised—Jordan liked to think of himself as a great ladies' man.

"What do you mean, they had to put you to bed?" he asked. He was jealous again and couldn't figure out why she would tell him something like this. She was impatient with his question.

"Oh c'mon," she said. "Don't start in. I was drunk. I couldn't have found my way to my apartment by myself if I tried."

"So what do you mean—they put you to bed? You mean they undressed you?"

"It was nothing. Martin has seen me naked a million times. It was no heavy thing."

"What about Jordan? He must have enjoyed himself," he said. She hesitated for a second.

"Oh, he didn't even come in. He waited for Martin by the elevator," she said.

"Sure. Right. Paul Jordan gallantly passed up the opportunity to undress you so he could wait by the elevator. Sounds just like him."

"That's what happened," she said.

"You just finished telling me you were so drunk you didn't know what was happening. But you seem real clear-headed now about Jordan being by the elevator."

"Why are you cross-examining me? I'm telling you it was nothing."

"Why did the two of them have to take you upstairs?" He was persistent. "Seems like Martin could have handled the job all by himself."

"I don't want to discuss it any more," she said.

"What if I told you that I went out on the town with Cathy and some other pretty ladies and got so drunk they had to bring me home, undress me and put me to bed. I suppose you'd think that was just great," he said.

"Let's just forget about it, okay?" she said. "It was nothing."

She loved Van Morrison, especially the double live album. He loved Van Morrison too, but that was the only l.p. of Morrison's he didn't have in his record collection. She had a copy and always played it when he was at her place. Her favorite cut was "Cyprus Avenue." "That goes right through me," she told him.

She insisted he borrow the record and listen to it. He agreed to borrow it, but he really didn't like borrowing things from people. He couldn't be as free with other people's things as with his own.

So he didn't play it. It wasn't that he consciously avoided playing it. It just never seemed like a good idea. He felt pressured to listen to it, as though she might make him take an exam on the record as soon as he gave it a good listen.

After he had the record at his place for a few weeks, she said, "You never listen to that record, do you?"

"I just haven't gotten around to it yet," he said.

"Well, look, if you're not going to play it, I might as well take it back. I love that record."

"I'll play it," he said.

"Well, obviously you're not that into it, so why don't I just take it back?" she said. He told her she should take it back if she missed it that much.

She loved the ballet. He never liked ballet. He became very lower-class whenever ballet or opera were mentioned. High Culture made him uncomfortable. She said, "Ballet is so beautiful. It's the human body at its most graceful. You don't know what you're missing."

They went to see "The Turning Point" and he hated it. "It wasn't the ballet at all," he said. "In fact, I thought the dance scenes were the best thing in the movie. But I thought the movie was terrible. I mean, I just didn't care whether the Anne Bancroft and Shirley Maclaine characters made the Right Choices in Life. And the movie didn't make me care. That's why it didn't work." He thought she agreed with him.

But then she told him she had seen it again.

"You're kidding—you saw it again?" he said.

"I don't think it's that bad a movie. I love the dance parts," she said.

He was angry. They hadn't seen each other in three or four days because she said she would be busy. He couldn't believe that one of the things she'd be busy doing was seeing that movie again.

"I thought you were real busy," he said.

"Well, a friend came by and we wanted to go out and that was the easiest thing to do," she said.

"What friend?" he asked.

"Nobody you know," she said.

"A woman friend or a guy?"

"Look, it was a guy. But it's no threat to you, believe me."

"So who is he then?" he said.

"If you have to know, it was Michael, the guy I was engaged to. But we broke up over three years ago," she said. "We don't sleep together or anything."

They both liked "The Last Waltz." She thought Robbie Robertson was a little too slick, he thought Robertson was okay. They agreed Van Morrison was great. But they both thought he looked smaller and older than their impression of him. He said he thought Dylan was a genius at taking his old songs and making them totally new.

After he had known her for only a short time, he wrote a poem for her and mailed it to her. It was a poem about how special she was to him and how he thought great things were in store for them. The first time he saw her after he sent her the poem, she told him how moved she had been by it. She almost cried, she said.

And a few days later he got a poem from her in the mail. It was "The Dawn" by William Butler Yeats. She copied the poem out by hand and at the bottom of the page wrote "my hands are cold." She was a big fan of Yeats. He knew he was supposed to recognize the poem right away, but he didn't. He thought at first it looked like Shakespeare. A writer he knew called him soon after he got the poem, and he asked the writer if he recognized it. The writer told him it was a Yeats poem. He pretended that he had pretty much figured out already that it was Yeats. But he was relieved to have the poem identified before he was to see her again.

He was disappointed that she hadn't said anything more significant or romantic than "my hands are cold."

She told him how much she liked his body. "Your skin is so soft," she said. "I know a lot of women who'd like to have skin like yours."

"It's just your typical working-class Irish Catholic body with a little German thrown in," he said.

"I love your long legs," she said.

"They're all yours," he said.

"You're the man of my dreams," she said.

She got a part-time job at a small bookstore called "Blueberry Hill Books" because the gallery didn't pay enough. He used to visit her there and afterwards she would tell him how he lit the place up for her when he came to visit. "I can't take my eyes off you," she said.

They were in the back room of the bookstore. She was on a break and they were talking. "Meeting you is like discovering a new world," she told him. He felt very blessed. He held her close to him and told her he had been waiting to meet her all his life.

It was after they had been together three months that he began to realize she must be involved with someone else. She was always "busy" and he usually saw her only once a week. And one time she told him they couldn't make love because she was "sore."

He began to get more and more jealous. They had spent the afternoon together one day in January and he invited her to stay for dinner but she said she wasn't hungry and had to go to the gallery anyway. A while after she left, he wanted to talk to her. He called the gallery but she wasn't there. Then he called her house. Someone else answered and told him she was eating dinner.

"I thought you were going to the gallery?" he said when she got on the phone.

"I decided to come home instead," she said. "I hardly spend any time here anymore."

"I thought you weren't hungry," he said.

"It was my night to cook," she said.

"Why do you lie to me all the time?" he asked. "You

34

could have just told me you had to go home and cook dinner. I wouldn't have had any trouble with that. But instead you tell me you're not hungry and you have to work at the gallery. That's pointless. You could just tell me the truth."

"I change my mind a lot. You better get used to that. I say I'm going to do something and I mean it, but then I'm out on the street and I change my mind and decide to do something else," she said.

"Don't bullshit me, please."

"Why don't you give it a rest?" she said.

He called her back and said he was very upset and wanted to talk to her. She came over and they had a long and painful conversation. She told him she was involved with two other men, but one was part of a relationship that was ending after four years and the other—the guy who lived in her house—was leaving for Europe in six weeks.

"What do you expect out of this relationship?" she asked.

"Everything," he said.

She told him she thought he was very brave to say that.

He took her to New York for a few days. On the train ride up, they took turns going to the bathroom to smoke pot. She had her big sketchbook with her and did three or four drawings during the trip. He brought a mayonnaise jar filled with Amaretto. After an hour they were both feeling high and slightly drunk and began kissing and touching each other. There weren't many people on the train, so he wasn't as self-conscious as he would normally be about such "public displays of affection," as he called it. She said to him on the train, "We have a very sexual relationship, you know."

He saved up two hundred dollars for the trip to New York so they could take cabs everywhere and eat out. He also wanted to buy things for her. They went to a used-clothes store on Canal Street and he bought her a beautiful black coat that fit her perfectly. She said she had been waiting years for a coat like this one. He told her she looked like a movie star in it.

They went to a lot of galleries in Soho. She was very excited by New York. She was impressed that he was a native New Yorker and knew his way around. He took her to the de Kooning show at the Guggenheim because de Kooning was her favorite painter. They checked out a Larry Rivers show at a gallery in mid-town. At one show in Soho, they found themselves in a strange room with a neon sign saying "Hotel Valparaiso." The entrance to the room was an opening about four feet high. They felt very aroused at being alone in this room and almost wound up making love. "You have such amazing eyes," she told him. "So do you," he said. "I've always fallen for brown eyes."

After the night in January when he told her he expected "everything," they broke up. He couldn't take her involvement with the two other men. He told her he was tired of feeling slighted and jealous constantly and of her being "busy" all the time. He gave her the choice of staying with him and dropping the others or breaking up.

She decided it would be better if they broke up. She told him she was not into "attachment."

"What do you mean?" he asked.

"I've had it with attachment," she said. "It's not where it's at. I want to be free. It's easy for a woman to get wrapped up in the life of some man. I want to be independent, live my own life."

"I think freedom means knowing how you're not free," he said. "You can't be free and independent unless you can accept what your needs are. Everybody is dependent. If you want to be strong you have to recognize your weaknesses."

"Not for me," she said.

"You're human too," he said.

"Yeah, it's easy for you to talk about accepting your weaknesses and all that—you're very together, you like your work, you got a nice place, good friends. It's different for women—they have to work a lot harder to be as together as that."

"Life is hard for all of us," he said.

"You know what I'm saying," she said.

"Yeah, I know what you're saying," he said.

But after a few days he couldn't take not seeing her and wanted to try again. She came over to his place and they had a long talk.

"Let's try again," he said. "I don't want to lose you. I'll try to accept the situation."

"I don't know," she said. "I'm not sure I can give you what you want."

"Why don't you think about it for a few days and we can get together on Monday and talk again."

"I'm not optimistic," she said.

"But we're great together," he said, "when it's working."

That Monday they got together at the Villa for a drink. It was a freezing cold day and the streets were deserted. The Villa was nearly empty. They talked for a long time. She said she couldn't stand walking past his building without being able to go up to see him. He had become so much a part of her life, she said. He told her he had been going crazy at the thought that they would not see each other again, not sleep together.

They went back to his place and he cooked some lunch for them. "You mean more to me than you'll ever know," she said.

She moved out of the house and into an efficiency he

helped her find. He looked through his apartment for things to give her. He gave her some plates, glasses, cups, towels, and an old quilt he had bought years ago. He helped her move. She had stopped seeing the other two men, but she borrowed a van from one of them for the move. He felt strange being in the other man's car. She told him she had been involved with Charles, the man who owned the van, for four years and that she and Charles once drove cross-country in this same van. All the tapes they played on the trip were still in the van, mostly stuff by The Band.

One night, a few months after she moved into the efficiency, she told him that Charles had visited her by surprise and asked her to marry him. He thought that was incredible.

The other guy, Henry, had moved out of the house he once shared with her and had gone to Europe as planned. But Michael, the man she had been engaged to years before—the one she saw "The Turning Point" with—was still in town. He was a lawyer. And a few weeks after Charles's proposal, Michael came by her place and, like Charles, he too asked her to marry him.

"So, did you say yes?" he asked jokingly.

"Are you kidding? I can't imagine having sex with him. I don't even remember what it was like."

"What's the story with these guys?" he asked. "I mean, you broke up with this guy three years ago and he knows you're involved with me—and he asks you to marry him?"

"I don't know," she said. "We were childhood sweethearts. We were the first for each other. For seven years."

She had given him a photograph of herself. In it, she was wearing a black silk slip and a straw hat. It wasn't a very good photograph, but she still looked beautiful. He framed it and put it up. When she moved into the efficiency, she asked him for a photograph. He gave her his favorite picture of himself. He thought the photograph revealed his intensity. She stuck it to her wall with masking tape. She had many drawings and photographs taped to her wall.

One day he came by for her. They were going to The Empress, their favorite Chinese restaurant, for dinner. Both of them loved Chinese food. One of the dishes they always ordered was Chicken and Walnuts in Plum Sauce. She used chopsticks and he used a fork. When he came by to pick her up, he noticed right away that his picture was no longer on her wall.

"Aha," he said. "I see you took down my picture. Does this mean we're through?" He was trying to be funny, but he was hurt.

"It gets so hot in here, everything keeps falling down," she said. He looked around and saw she was right. Pieces of tape were curling off the wall.

"So just tape it back up," he suggested.

"I will. It fell down just before. I haven't gotten around to it yet."

"It doesn't take much. A little piece of fresh tape," he said. She got angry and impatient.

"Don't give me a hard time, okay? I don't control the weather."

He was still amazed that Charles had asked her to marry him and months after the proposal, he asked her about him.

"I was in love with him for years," she said. "But he didn't love me. It drove me crazy. You wouldn't have recognized me then. I was very domestic. And innocent."

"So what happened?" he asked.

"For a year he wouldn't make love to me. Every night I wanted it, but he wasn't interested. Finally, I gave up. But it took a long time for me to break out of it. When I finally started coming to life again, the tables were turned. He started falling in love with me. But it was too late by then."

"That's the way it goes. You get what you want when you don't want it anymore," he said.

"I guess," she said.

"Well, I'm glad you turned him down," he said.

"Are you kidding?—you're the man of my dreams, remember?"

"Your waking hours too, I hope."

"I told you already, I never had it so good."

"You don't think I'm a pervert anymore?" he said.

"You've liberated me sexually. That's the truth," she said.

"You ain't seen nothing yet," he said. She laughed.

"I know," she said, "we deserve each other, right?"

His picture never reappeared on her wall. So one day he took down the picture of her in the black silk slip and stuck it behind a bookcase. When she noticed her photograph was no longer on the wall, she was mad.

"What happened to the picture of me?" she asked.

"It fell off the wall," he said. She ignored him.

"Why did you take it down?" she demanded.

"Why did you take mine down?" he asked.

"I told you, the tape won't stay on."

"Yeah, right," he said.

"So, a little retaliation, hah?" she said.

"I told you, it just fell down. I haven't gotten around to putting it back up."

"You're not funny," she said. The next day he put her picture back on the wall.

She quit her jobs at the bookstore and the gallery and got a new job as a waitress at a local café. He then began picking her up every night when she got off and walking her back to his place. She would call him at about one thirty in the morning and tell him she was ready to leave and he would put on his shoes and practically race to the restaurant to meet her. They were both paranoid and he didn't want her walking around alone late at night.

He didn't like the idea of her being a waitress. She would always tell him stories about men customers. But she was never direct. She'd start to say something about some customer bothering her or trying to pick her up, but then she'd drop the subject. He always wanted to know the details, even though the thought of her on public display made him jealous.

"I hate this job," she said. "I hate those stupid men staring at me. I always know when they're watching me and I feel so violated. Some of them aren't too subtle either."

"What do they do?" he asked.

"Oh, nothing. Don't worry. They're harmless. It's just a pain. Let's talk about something else, okay?"

He stopped by the restaurant her first night on the job to give her some moral support. It was very busy and she looked hassled. He caught her eye and waved. She came up to him and he said, "How's it going?" "It's real busy," she said.

He sat down to have a cup of coffee. He saw her talking to another waitress and pointing at him. The other waitress came over and asked if she could help him.

He thought he had sat at one of her tables and was surprised when the other waitress arrived to wait on him. He ordered a cup of coffee. He watched her and tried to get her attention. But she wouldn't even look in his direction and after ten or fifteen minutes, he felt like he was sinking inside. She was ignoring him completely. He stayed a while longer, left some money on the table, and walked out.

"You acted like you never saw me before," he said to her later. "I couldn't believe it. I felt really ridiculous."

"It was so busy, I didn't want to get distracted."

"But you wouldn't even look in my direction. I didn't expect you to be all over me. But I didn't think you'd act like we never met," he said.

"You're right," she said. "I'm sorry."

"But why would you do that?" he asked. She started crying.

"I don't know what's wrong with me," she said. "Sometimes things happen in my head that I can't explain. I cut everything off. I cut everyone off. I'm not trying to make excuses. I don't know why I ignored you. I'm sorry."

She said she wanted to put make-up on him and he said he'd go along with that. So one night she brought all her make-up over. They both got stoned and she started working on his face.

She darkened his eyes, put powder and rouge on his cheeks, and lipstick on his lips. She handed him a mirror and he looked at himself.

"Pretty weird," he said.

"Do you like it?"

"It's strange," he said.

He was frightened of what he looked like. First, he thought he looked perverted and decadent, like Joel Grey in "Cabaret." Then he thought his face made him look as though he were embalmed.

"I'm so addicted to you," she said.

"I'll bet you say that to all the guys," he said.

"No. You're special. You're always doing things for me. Giving me presents, cooking all the time. I should cook for you. I'm a great cook."

"Prove it," he said.

"I will. Listen, my mother taught me all the things a girl should know. How to cook, sew, you name it."

"Any time you feel inspired to cook for us, be my guest."

"I'm really terrible to you," she said.

"No you're not," he said.

"It's true. You do everything. I never do anything for you. Except give you a hard time. Sometimes I don't know why you bother with me," she said.

"Lust," he said.

"No, really. I should treat you better."

"You mean you weren't this way with your other boyfriends?" he asked.

"Henry I gave a real hard time to. He got it worse than anyone. I think because he was younger than me." ⁱ

"What about Charles?" he asked.

"Are you kidding? I didn't dare. Charles doesn't take any shit from anyone. He sure didn't take any from me," she said. Then she realized what she had said and the two of them froze.

"And I do, right?" he said.

"That's not what I meant," she said. "It was different with him. I was a different person."

The day she moved out of the house and into the efficiency, he gave her keys to his apartment. He told her she should give him a key to her new building.

"I don't like that neighborhood," he said. "If I don't have a key, I'll have to yell up for you to let me in. I'd prefer not to do that."

"I'll get you one," she said. "I'll talk to the resident manager."

He stayed at her place one night soon after she moved in. She had a single mattress on the floor and one pillow. She claimed the pillow for herself because it was her place. When they got into bed she began to squirm around and act exasperated.

"What's wrong?" he asked her.

"You're taking up too much space," she said.

"No I'm not," he said. "Look, I'm taking up exactly half the bed." He made an imaginary line down the center of the bed.

"You keep inching over to my half," she said.

He lay in bed feeling uncomfortable and unwelcome. He couldn't fall asleep and could tell she was still awake. He felt very resentful. At his place, he always tried to make her happy.

He got out of bed and started putting his clothes on.

"What are you doing?" she asked.

"I'm going back to my place," he said.

"Why? What are you talking about?"

"I can't fall asleep here."

"Don't go," she said. "I want you to stay."

"It doesn't feel that way," he said.

She never got him a key to her building. He was surprised. He didn't expect her to give him a key to her apartment. He knew she would see that as a threat to her freedom and independence. But he didn't think she would have any problem with giving him a key to her building. She told him it was a special kind of key. She had tried a few places that made keys, but they said they couldn't make a copy of it.

"Why don't you just tell the landlord you need a new key," he said. "Tell him you lost yours."

"That's an idea," she said.

They stayed most of the time at his place. She was usually asleep when he came home from a job. She was sometimes very cold towards him when he got into bed. The first time that happened, he was taken aback. He remembered getting into bed and trying to hold her for a moment. But she wouldn't let him touch her. She made a face and rolled away from him. She put her knees up to block his attempts to embrace her.

Whenever he visited her apartment she acted suspicious

towards him. He figured she was frightened he would see some souvenir of her romantic past that she had forgotten to hide away. She kept a close eye on him when he was in her apartment. If he looked around, she would say, "What are you looking for?" He got into the habit of sitting in her armchair by the window and getting up only to go to the bathroom.

"You don't like it here, do you?" she asked him.

"No. It's nice. It's a nice place," he said.

"You always act like you don't really want to be here."

"I want to be here. That's why I'm here."

"I mean, you seem stiff here," she said.

"I guess sometimes I feel you're not too open with me. You seem suspicious of me. I'm afraid to look around when I'm here," he said.

"No—I want you to like it here," she said. "I bought stuff especially because you were coming over. There's cake and apple juice and Coke. In honor of you."

He was in "The Fiddle and the Bow" with his best friend Jack Harte. Harte was drinking Glenfiddich and he was drinking Jameson's and water.

"Jack, she drives me crazy. I think the future looks dim for this romance."

"I don't know. I talked to her today on the street and the impression she gave me was that she's totally crazy about you," his friend said.

"What did she say?" he asked.

"It wasn't so much what she said as how she said it. It was the way she talked about you. You and her. In my opinion, I'd say you were stuck with that girl for a long time to come, like it or not." Harte was from the old country.

"Well, she knows what to say to you—you're my closest friend. I bet her friends get a different impression."

"My advice to you would be just stick with it and see

what happens," Harte said. "I don't think you have anything to worry about. Just trust yourself."

"I might as well. She doesn't."

"Relax. I think you don't want to believe it's working."

"No. It's more complicated than that."

"These are difficult times we live in," Harte said. "Did
you ever hear that Chinese curse?"

"What is it?"

"May you live in interesting times," his friend said.

"You have a beautiful body," he told her.

"No, *you* have a beautiful body. You have the body of a
sixteen-year-old," she said.

"Yeah, I keep it in the refrigerator," he said. She laughed.

"You turn me on," she said. "Sometimes just thinking
about you gets me aroused."

"The same is true for me, you know," he said.

"Then everything's perfect," she said.

"You look really beautiful right now," he said. "I wish I
had a camera."

"What would you do—send the results to *Playboy?*"

"That's a good idea," he said. "You sure got the body for
it and we could pick up some extra dough."

"*We?*—you got a frog in your pocket?" she said.

"I'll be your agent."

"You know, you're the first man I ever went out with
who didn't hide his dirty magazines. I always told myself
I'd never go out with a man who read that stuff. But here I
am," she said.

"Another first, huh?"

"That's right," she said. "And you're also the cutest
and sexiest."

"And the tallest, the oldest, and funniest, right?"

"You got it," she said.

*

He told her about an episode of "The Twilight Zone" he remembered from when he was about seventeen. At the time he was living alone with his father in New York, in the apartment he grew up in. His older brothers and sisters had gotten married and moved out. His grandfather and his mother had died a year earlier.

"That place was haunted," he said. "There was a full-length mirror at the end of the long hall that ran through the apartment, so when you came in the front door and looked to the right, you'd see yourself coming in."

"Mirrors give me the creeps," she said. "I don't have any mirrors in my place. Except for the medicine cabinet."

"When my mother was really sick, she had to hold on to the walls in the hall to get from one end of the apartment to the other. After she died I used to think I still saw her walking down the hall holding the wall. From the corner of my eye."

"I don't know how you went through all that at that age," she said.

"But this one night when I was seventeen my father went somewhere for the weekend and I was alone in the apartment," he said. "And I put the t.v. on. I started watching 'The Twilight Zone.' It was all about this middle-aged guy in the Navy. It opens with him on a ship somewhere out on the ocean. The time is supposed to be now. Then he, and the other guys on the ship, begin to hear this rhythmic noise—I think it was a kind of clang—coming from somewhere in the ocean. Underneath them."

His eyes began to water as he told the story. She had once told him that she was afraid of "The Twilight Zone" when she was a kid. And she seemed a little nervous now as he told this story.

"So, what was the noise?" she asked.

"Well, they decided to go down and see where the noise was coming from. Meanwhile, the middle-aged guy starts getting more and more weird the longer the sound goes on. You know right away there's some connection between him and the noise."

"What was it?" she asked.

"Well, they go down and they find this sunken submarine. An American submarine destroyed during World War Two. And the noise seems to be coming from inside it. And guess what?"

"What?" she said.

"It turns out to be the submarine the guy served on during the war. When it was hit, he was the only survivor."

"Yeah. So?"

"All I remember is the guy down there in the submarine poking around and getting more and more freaked out as they get closer to the noise. Finally, he's in this little room. I think he opens a door, a closet or something, and there's this mirror he's facing." He had to stop and dry his eyes.

"I don't know if I want to hear the rest of this," she said.

"So he's standing there looking in the mirror, right? And on the other side of the mirror, looking back at him, are all his dead shipmates from the war. And they're all smiling at him and beckoning to him with their fingers."

"Oh, God," she said. "I'm glad I missed that one."

"I'm not even sure if that was the end," he said. "I switched the t.v. off and went down and stood on the stoop till dawn. It was raining. I smoked a lot and got very tired. But I didn't want to go back to that apartment that night."

Two years before she met him, she told him, she got very sick. She was sick for a whole year, she said. They didn't know what it was. Maybe mono. Maybe hypoglycemia. She couldn't do anything. She could hardly get out of bed. Charles took care of her, she said, and lent her thousands of dollars to meet her expenses. Her parents were very worried. She slowly got better, but still had to be careful.

"You seem so healthy to me," he said. "You don't smoke, you don't use sugar, you keep yourself in good shape. But you're always getting sick."

"You get sick more than me," she said. She thought he was suggesting her sicknesses were imaginary and that annoyed her.

"Yeah, but when I get sick, I deserve it," he said.

She told him she was cured finally by Dr. Chen, an acupuncturist. She recommended he see Dr. Chen about his allergies. He said he would try anything.

Dr. Chen hardly examined him when he eventually went to see him.

"I can tell from your skin what your problems are," the doctor said. "Some breathing problems. Your kidneys might be a problem too." The doctor asked him some questions about his family history and lifestyle. As he answered the questions he could feel the doctor studying him, looking for clues about him.

Finally, the doctor asked him matter-of-factly, "Do you have fear?"

He was surprised the doctor would ask him something like that.

"What do you want anyway?" she asked him. They were both angry. She had gone on a date with some guy she used to work with. She told him it was nothing to worry about—the guy had a beautiful wife he was totally in love with. But the day after the date she told him it turned out that the guy and his wife had split and the guy asked her at dinner if she would start going out with him.

"I guess I want you to be more enthusiastic about being involved with me," he said. "You go out on these dates with guys who are obviously interested in you romantically or sexually—and don't pretend you're too naive to see that—or you tell me you don't want to see me for a few days, or whatever, and it just makes me feel like you're less than enthusiastic about me."

He remembered back a long time ago, when she first started working at the bookstore. They were in the back room one evening, lying on the floor kissing. And he told her how much she meant to him. Then she told him she didn't want to hurt him. She said he should watch his expectations.

He didn't take lightly what she said. He thought to himself that if somebody says they don't want to hurt you, that means they're going to hurt you. And if they tell you to watch your expectations, what they're really saying is you better not have any expectations.

But he took the advice of his friend Jack and stayed with it. And at times it seemed like it might all come together.

"I don't know what you mean by 'enthusiastic,'" she said. "I'm not sleeping with anyone else. I spend almost all my time with you. I didn't know this guy and his wife split up."

He didn't say anything.

"Oh, great. So now you're going to sulk," she said. "My father always did that. That was his big move when he didn't get his way."

"I'm not sulking and please don't pull your father trip on me," he said.

"Look, I don't know what to tell you. You seem to have this idea of progress, like you think we're going to get closer and closer. Well, maybe this is as close as we're going to get. Maybe this is as deep as it will go and it'll last another year or so and that's it," she said.

"What are you saying?" he asked.

"Just what I said," she replied.

"So, you think we got a good year ahead of us and that's it?"

"Maybe. I don't know," she said.

"I think we really are different," he said. "You're right—I guess I do expect things to get deeper and closer. It really surprises me that you would say something like that—that we've peaked and maybe have another year to play it out."

"Well, there's no use fooling ourselves," she said.

She woke him up in the middle of the night once.

"Stop snoring," she said.

"I was snoring?"

"Like a motorcycle. It's driving me crazy."

"I'm sorry. I didn't even know I snored."

"So now you know."

"Nobody's ever said anything to me in the past about snoring," he said.

"Please, don't blame it on me," she said.

"No, I mean, you'd think somebody would have said something before this," he said.

"You mean somebody out of all those hundreds you've been to bed with?"

His father used to snore. You could hear it throughout the apartment. But everyone in his family knew that to stop him all you had to say was "Dad, stop snoring" and he'd stop, without ever waking up.

He suggested to her that rather than wake him up, she try the method his family used on his father.

"Just tell me to stop snoring," he said to her. "But be firm. Tell me—don't just ask me to stop."

But a few nights later she woke him up again out of a deep sleep.

"Look, you've got to stop snoring. I can't sleep. I put the pillow over my head. But nothing works." He was angry. He didn't want her to get in the habit of waking him up out of a sound sleep.

"Did you try just telling me to stop in my sleep?"

"It didn't work. You kept on snoring."

"This is crazy—I've got to sleep too. You can't be waking me up all the time," he said.

"I woke you up because you were making it impossible for me to sleep," she said.

"Look, next time why don't you just pretend it's music. Make believe it's a lullaby," he said.

They were in The Empress for dinner. She was dressed in a very alluring outfit—a lacey white halter top that highlighted her breasts and left her belly bare, and a black skirt. He didn't like her dressing too daringly on the street. He told her he didn't like it when she attracted the attention of other men. He didn't want to have to deal with all that. So she wore a blue work shirt over the halter top and took it off when they got to the The Empress.

"I'm so wrapped up in you," she said. "You're the most romantic man I've ever met."

"Think so?"

"You know it," she said. "Most men don't buy presents and write poems for their girl friends."

"Most men don't wind up with women like you— you're the most beautiful woman I've ever gone out with," he said.

"Oh yeah? What about the actress—Janet or whatever her name is?" He had once been involved with a beautiful actress who was now beginning to make the Big Time in New York. "I'll bet she was something—how was she, huh?"

"She was fine," he said.

"What do you mean, 'fine'?" she asked.

"We liked each other," he said.

"Was she as good as me?"

"No. No comparison," he said.

"Why not?"

"You smell much better than she did," he said.

"You smell like carnations, you know," she said.

"You smell like bacon and eggs, easy over," he said.

"Well, I wouldn't want to compete with her. I don't even think about her—it makes me jealous," she said.

"You have nothing to worry about. I broke up with her six months before I met you. And I don't think there would be much between me and Janet now."

"Were you in love with her?"

"I don't know—it was a strange relationship. We didn't even see that much of each other. And we never talked about our romantic pasts. It was like "Last Tango in Paris." Except that we did know each other's names. At least I guess that was her name. Janet Ross."

"Ooo, stop! I don't even like to hear you say her name," she said.

"Sorry," he said.

"You know what else you do that no other man I've gone out with ever did?" she said.

"What's that?"

"You talk dirty."

"You like that, huh? What a pervert."

"I think you're very brave," she said. He didn't know what to say.

"What do you mean?" he asked.

"I just think you're very brave. The way you live your life. You've thought out a lot of things and you live by that. I admire that a lot," she said.

"I'm not brave," he said. "I'm a coward."

"What will you be like when you're famous?" she asked. "You'll probably drop me for some starlet."

"You mean I'm not famous? I thought I was famous."

"I mean when you're even more famous than you are now," she said, playing along with him.

"More famous than I am now?" he said. "Impossible."

"You might be," she said. "I look at you sometimes and think you'll be very famous some day."

"Cover of *Rolling Stone,* stuff like that?"

"Yeah, stuff like that," she said.

"Don't hold your breath."

"I bet it happens."

"Well, don't worry. I'm a very tenacious person," he said. "And very consistent."

He met his friend Jack at Mirsky's Pharmacy. Mirsky's was a combination drugstore, luncheonette, and news-stand with a Southern charm that made it seem anachronistic. They bought cigarettes and the newspaper and went back to his place.

"What have you been up to?" Jack asked him.

"I've been reading Poe. I read somewhere that 'The Murders in the Rue Morgue' was the first detective story, so I decided to check it out."

"How is it?"

"I'm not finished it yet. I guess I read it a long time ago, probably in high school, but I don't remember. I can't believe the direction it's taking, though."

"Which is what?" Jack asked.

"Well, before I stopped last night, all the clues pointed to the possibility that an orangutan was the murderer. I didn't want to ruin the suspense, so I saved the rest for today. I'm still expecting Poe to come up with something a little more believable. I don't want to face the thought that the American detective story starts out with an orangutan murderer. It's too ridiculous," he said.

"We should write a series of detective stories in which the murderer is *always* an orangutan," Jack suggested.

"I used to live right near Poe's house in the Bronx. I swear, they must have all been midgets in those days. The place is tiny."

"Maybe we should make our orangutans very small ones. Midget orangutans, no bigger than cats, terrorizing the entire city," his friend said.

"Start without me," he said.

"How's the lovelife?" Jack asked.

"I don't know, man. I start thinking everything's okay. Then the barn door hits me in the face again."

"What happened?"

"She stood me up last night."

"Again?"

"That's right. She was supposed to come over when the bookstore closed at seven. I waited around till seven thirty, then I walked over there and they told me she split around ten after with Martin. I was feeling very crazy. I couldn't believe she would treat me like this. I walked around for a while, stopped at the liquor store and picked up some booze, and headed back to my place. Then I saw her half a block ahead of me."

"So, what did you do?"

"Well, first I was just going to disappear and let her arrive at my place with me not there. But that would be retaliation, which she's always accusing me of. So I caught up with her."

"What'd she say?"

"She confessed to everything, admitted she was wrong and I was right and said she'd never do it again."

"The plot thins," Jack said.

"And she told me again there's nothing between her and Martin. They're just friends and she has trouble making friends and I have to understand that, etcetera etcetera."

"Did she try to explain what happened?"

"She said she tried to call me to tell me she'd be late but my line was busy and she really wanted to go to this art opening Martin told her about and it turned out there was food at the opening and they decided to eat and she didn't realize how late it was, blah blah blah and so on. The usual."

"Listen, I know you're in love with her, but maybe you should check out some of these other ladies around. What about Barbara? I wouldn't kick her out of bed. You should call her up, make a date," Jack said.

"I've never turned a woman down," Jack once told him. "It's bad karma."

He envied that attitude. He was the opposite. To most people, especially those with a romantic interest in him, he was very aloof. He felt he had to be overwhelmingly attracted to someone before he would even consider getting involved.

Neither approach seemed too successful. His friend Jack spent almost two years with a deep frown fixed on his face— the result of an elaborate, prolonged rejection by a young woman he was in love with. The two friends worked out an ornate system of theories about affairs of the heart. Although the theories shifted and contradicted each other depending on the situation at any given time, one ruling principle emerged from their discussions: expect the worst.

He did not have much optimism about his present circumstances. She was a beautiful woman, more spoiled than he and at least as self-absorbed. She was used to being in control. She was used to rejecting men who had been in love with her for years. By now, she was also used to her rejected "beaux" turning up at her door years later and proposing marriage. He knew she would not surrender her free-wheeling power over the male population just to make him happy.

He called her and she said she would be busy for the next few days.

"Oh, c'mon, not again," he said. "What are you doing this time that's so important?"

"I don't want to talk about it," she said.

"Well, I do," he said. "There has to be some trust between us. I mean, I would consider it crazy and insulting if a friend were as remote as you. But we're lovers."

"I don't want to be answerable to you all the time," she said. "There are some things I want to do on my own."

"I tell you everything," he said. "And it doesn't make me feel threatened. If you care about somebody and trust them, then I don't see why telling them what you're doing is such a big deal."

"Look, I want to learn to exist on my own and I don't want to feel guilty about it. You're always guilt-tripping me," she said.

"And every time you do something that hurts me and I let you know about it, you get yourself off the hook by accusing me of guilt-tripping you. So I have to shut up lest I prove you're right. And I wind up feeling it's me that's giving you a hard time instead of vice versa," he said.

He decided to take his friend's advice and call up Barbara for a date. He took her to The Empress and they talked about New York. Barbara had been living in New York for the past two years. He thought she was pretty attractive, but she seemed passionless to him. And very middle-class. After they finished eating, they went to his place for coffee, then he walked her home.

"The next time I'll treat you," Barbara said when they got to her place.

"It's a deal," he said. But they never went out again.

He didn't tell her about his date with Barbara until a long time later. He avoided telling her about other women he thought were attractive or about women who came on to him at jobs he played. She was all he wanted and he didn't want to spoil anything by making her jealous.

"I'm very jealous too," she told him once.

"Not as bad as me," he said.

"No, you don't know. I get very jealous. You're up there on a stage playing all the time with all these little groupies all over you. Don't think I'm not aware of that."

"I've been completely faithful to you," he said.

"Yeah, I'll bet."

"It's true."

"There's been nobody else?"

"In the whole time I've known you, I went out once with someone else," he said.

"You did?" She was surprised.

"It was nothing. Very brief. No sex. I didn't really enjoy it," he said.

"Who was she?"

"It doesn't matter."

"C'mon, tell me who it was. I want to know."

"Look, the first three months we were involved you were sleeping with two other guys and going out on dates with every other man who looked at you twice. I didn't ask any questions. So I got pissed off one time when you told me you'd be 'busy' and made a date with someone else. It doesn't matter who. Nothing happened," he said.

"Tell me who it was."

"No."

"Was it Barbara? I bet it was Barbara. God! She is such a twerp. I'd be disappointed in you if it was her."

"It wasn't Barbara," he said.

"I bet her shit is pink, the sweet little thing."

It was the first time he lied to her. It made him feel guilty, even though he felt she had sinned against their relationship much more seriously and frequently than he had. When they were getting to know each other, she told him she sometimes lied. "If the situation demands it," she said. "I'll lie. But only if I have to."

"If it wasn't Barbara, who was it? Was it Julie?" she asked. Julie was a good friend of his. Both of them liked

Julie—she was a poet and painter, very attractive, with striking blue eyes.

"No. It wasn't Julie," he said.

"I bet you'd like to take a little fling with her. She's beautiful and sexy, like a kitten," she said.

"We're just friends. You know that. Anyway, Julie's in love with Carlos and I don't interfere with other people's relationships," he said.

"You're such a saint," she said.

"Thanks," he said.

"C'mon, tell me who you went out with."

"No. Forget it."

"*Please* tell me."

"You really want to know?"

"Yes," she said.

"It was an orangutan," he said.

He first met her on a "Moonlight Cruise" on the Chesapeake Bay months before the rainy day when he visited her house and they became lovers. She was the guitar player's date for the Moonlight Cruise. She wore tight blue jeans and a faded pink pull-over. When she wasn't looking his way, he couldn't take his eyes off her. He stood jammed onto the little bandstand with the rest of the band and had to fight against the swerves of the ship. But he never played better.

He didn't go near her all night. He didn't know what was going on between her and the guitar player, but he envied him anyway. They all went up to the top deck on a break and started singing old rock 'n' roll songs. She stood in front of him at the railing. The guitar player had his arm around her waist and he would have given anything to trade places with him.

But he didn't even try to talk to her. That was his "code." You stay off other people's territory. She seemed oblivious to him anyway. That made it easier for him to pretend that he didn't even notice her.

But he wanted her badly. She had long black hair that reached all the way down her back. And brown eyes. Her lips were full and inviting. She seemed strong and healthy and classically beautiful to him. The sexiest woman he had ever seen. More beautiful than Janet Ross, even. But she made more than just a physical impression on him. The way she danced and talked captivated him. He was not attracted to most people, including the pretty ones.

"You know what really turns me on?" he once asked Jack Harte.

"What?"

"Intelligence. And depth. That's what gets me hooked."

"You mean stupidity doesn't drive you wild with desire?" his friend asked.

"That's right," he said.

After the boat docked, he began breaking down the equipment, packing up his instruments, and helping to haul everything to the cars. A middle-aged woman, who was drunk, fell into the water as she was disembarking. That caused quite a bit of concern and commotion. Almost all the passengers were drunk. The band members and their entourage were stoned as well. It had been a beautiful night, the water tranquil, the moon radiant, the people in good spirits. A very romantic setting that got his juices pumping. She sat with the guitar player near the bandstand. They were singing together. A Hank Williams song, "Lovesick Blues." Both of them had beautiful voices.

In the spirit of the evening, he was feeling pretty good. But as he heard them singing, a marked sadness took hold of him. He had broken up with Janet the actress nine months earlier. The summer before she had been his date when he played the Moonlight Cruise. For a long time, he had been feeling unlucky. Everything I touch falls apart, he thought.

The evening was almost over. Most of the band equipment had been brought ashore. He went back to the ship to see if he could find anything left to carry out. The girl and the guitar player were still there, sitting near the deserted bandstand talking. Except for a few people cleaning up around the bar, the two of them were the only ones left on board. He poked around the bandstand, pretending to be searching for any equipment he might have overlooked, but secretly checking out the happy couple. The guitar player noticed him.

"Time to get rolling, I guess," the guitar player said.

"Yeah. Now is the hour," he said. The guitar player got up and started packing his instruments.

He left them and went back out to the dock. The bass player had moved his station wagon to within a few feet of the pile of equipment—instruments, battered suitcases filled with microphones, two big Shure speakers, and the Vocalmaster head. Then the bass player went back on board to grab one last beer for the road. He was left to load all their stuff into the station wagon.

While he was loading up, the girl and the guitar player finally left the ship. When they got to the station wagon, the guitar player asked her if she wanted to wait there while he got his car or come with him.

"I'll wait here," she said.

He felt the excitement shoot through him. She now stood just a few feet from him. It was about two in the morning, the night still warm. The bay glimmered all around them. She looked breathtaking to him. But he knew he should be cool. The guitar player left to get his car.

"Hello," she said.

"Hi," he said. "How'd you like the boat ride?"

"It was great," she said. "I'm really glad I came. I've

been wanting to hear you guys for a long time."

"I'm glad you liked it."

"Did you see that woman fall in the water?" she asked.

"The curse of drink," he said. They both seemed nervous. He didn't know what to say to her. Then he realized he didn't know her name.

"What's your name?" he asked.

"Madeleine Green," she said. He said nothing for a moment as he looked at her and attached the name forever to her face.

"That's a beautiful name," he said. "Mine's Willie Flynn."

"I know," she said. "I saw a review of yours in the paper. I thought it was really good."

"Thanks," he said. "You live in town?"

"Yeah, on Capitol Hill. But I'm supposed to move next week to Dupont Circle."

"Then we'll be neighbors," he said. "Let's have lunch or something after you move."

"I'd like that a lot," she said.

"I love your name," Willie said. "It's really lovely."

The night they broke up for good almost a year later, they were both confused. Neither of them knew exactly why they were breaking up. She had come over to Willie's place and both of them were crying.

"Let me stay over, please," she said.

"No. That's crazy," he said. "If we've broken up, it would be crazy to spend the night together. It would just make it harder."

"Just one more time," she said. She was acting as though the break up were his idea.

"I think I'd rather be alone tonight," he said.

He walked her back to her apartment. They both continued to cry inconspicuously on the street.

"I'm afraid I'll never meet another man like you," she

said. He didn't say anything. When they got to her apartment building on Seventeenth Street, she said, "I'll miss you. A lot." The finality terrified Willie.

"Do you want to keep the door open and see what happens?" he said.

"Yeah," she said. "Let's keep the door open."

"Okay," he said.

He went back to his place, but couldn't sleep. He called Jack, waking him up, and arranged for him to feed his cat. In the morning he took a cab to Union Station and caught the Minuteman to New York. He wanted to spend some time with his old friends.

▼

TRIGGER RESPONSE

I LOVE CHRISTINE, but we have our problems. I hate
arguments. When she complains, I get angry. When she
cries, I fall apart. The guilt drives me up the walls.

My super, Mr. King, was up here a few days ago to fix a
leak in the bathroom. I brought him a beer while he was
working. He asked how things were going with "the girlfriend." Mr. King, like everybody else in the building, has
noticed that Christine now shares the apartment with me.

"Things are okay," I said. "We fight once in a while."

"Let me give you some advice, Mr. Carolan," he said.

"What?"

"If she steps out of line, give her a good boot where
she'll feel it."

"I don't get into that stuff, Mr. King," I said. "I'm a
pacifist."

"Pacifist, schmacifist," he said. "I'm telling you what to
do—a good kick where she'll feel it. It's the only way."

"I try to avoid that," I said. "I don't think violence
solves anything."

"Violence solves lots of things," he said. "My wife got her problems, Mr. Carolan. She can't have any more kids. Not that I want any more, believe me. We got five right now, which is plenty. But she got these problems and needs to see the doctor every time I turn around."

"I'm sorry to hear that."

"Not as sorry as me, Mr. Carolan," he said. "Between you and me, when I need it I know where to get it for five dollars. A man has to take care of his drives."

"Yeah, right," I said.

"But it's these doctors that get to me. They stink. They take your money and you're supposed to genuflect when they walk by."

"I'm not crazy about doctors either."

"The other day I took her to the hospital, you know? She wasn't doing too good. And I don't trust this doctor she sees. Very high and mighty. Always gives me the brush-off, with his nose in the air."

"A lot of them are like that."

"So I figured it was time to have a few words with His Holiness. I just took him aside and said, 'listen, Doctor, get one thing straight: if anything goes wrong with my wife, I'm coming back here and you know what I'm gonna do? I'm gonna wipe up the floor with you, Doctor. That's right. You're gonna wish you did the job right. So don't make any mistakes, understand?' "

"What did he say?"

"He didn't say anything, Mr. Carolan. But, let me tell you, nothing went wrong. And now his lordship treats me with respect. So, sometimes a little violence pays off."

It was Christine's idea that we live together. Personally, I thought we had a pretty good arrangement already. She lived a couple of blocks away at her parents' place, but spent most of her time here. We had our individual escape hatches. But she wanted to get away from the whole family trip. I don't blame her.

Her father is very authoritarian. I supported Paul O'Dwyer and Gene McCarthy in the last election. I actually worked for the O'Dwyer people, handing out flyers on Fordham Road, knocking on doors, all that stuff. Mr. Delaney, Christine's father, is a big admirer of Nixon. He has never forgiven me my left-wing sympathies.

One night just before the elections, I came by to pick up Christine. While I was waiting for her, I got into a discussion with her father about the war. An argument, actually. It got pretty heated and finally, when he thought I was getting the best of him, he looked at me and said, "Take off your hat when you're in this house." I still had my hat and coat on. I hate that kind of cheap paternalism, so I just walked out and waited for Christine on the street.

Christine pushed hard for cohabitation and eventually I gave in. Actually, I was more worried about confronting her parents than about us living together. But she insisted we had to go over there and lay our cards on the table. I dreaded it.

We sat in the living room with her parents and explained that we were going to live together. At first, her father tried to act reasonable.

"Just do one thing, that's all I ask," he said.

"What's that?" I said.

"Just go to the rectory with us and have a talk with the pastor. Before you make any decisions, just do that one thing."

"Look, Mr. Delaney, we know the Church's stand on what we're doing. I mean, between the two of us, we've got about thirty-five years of Catholic education."

"Just talk to him first."

"No, we don't want to do that," I said. "We've made up our minds."

Mr. Delaney was never one of my biggest fans. But after that night, I was through forever as far as he was concerned. He made Christine hand over her keys to the house. I thought that was really petty of him. And he forbade her brothers and her sister to set foot in my apartment. *Our* apartment now.

Christine got a job downtown at a graphics place. She hates it, but the money helps. My fellowship stipend doesn't go very far. But I'm not complaining. The fellowship beats working and so far it's helped keep thousands of miles between me and Vietnam. It's a National Defense Education Act grant. I had to sign a loyalty oath to get it.

I think I would do just about anything to stay out of the war. When I look deep inside myself, I realize I'm totally chicken. I would like to have the moral courage of someone like Dan Berrigan, but it's not in the cards. I was a follower of the Berrigan brothers for a while. I went to special liturgies and to Dan's poetry readings. I read everything they wrote. But finally my own moral cowardice made me feel like a hypocrite. I dropped out of the Berrigan movement. I don't want to go to Vietnam. But I don't want to go to jail either.

I know three guys who have been killed over there, in Nam. Eddie Fenton's death was the one that really got to me. We were in college together, but weren't good friends. Just acquaintances. I ran into him at a party the summer before last. Eddie was a nice guy, but no Einstein. I had heard that he got drafted. Somebody at the party told me. He was leaving for Fort Dix the next day. He spotted me from across the room and came up to me.

"Hey, Mike Carolan—how you doin'?"

"I beg your pardon?" I said.

"Mike Carolan, right?"

"You must be mistaken," I said. "That's not my name."
Eddie looked confused. I immediately felt guilty about

putting him on, but I couldn't seem to stop myself.

"Mike, c'mon, gimme a break," he said.

"My name isn't Mike."

"Hey, come off it, huh?"

"There seems to be somebody named Mike whom I resemble—since somebody else made the same mistake as you—but I assure you I'm not your friend Mike."

"You're putting me on, right?"

"No," I lied, staring right into his eyes. He laughed with embarrassment and walked away. "Sorry to bother you, pal," he said.

Months later, when I heard the news that Eddie Fenton was killed in Vietnam, my hands started shaking. I'm superstitious. I put the guy on, humiliated him, for a cheap laugh. Now he was dead. He was there only three days when he got hit. I pretend I don't believe in God. But I secretly do. And now, I thought, God will definitely punish me for what I did to Eddie and send me to Vietnam.

But then I think, no, the U.S. Army will never take me. I have asthma and can prove it. I'm pretty sure I have a hernia. And last year I went to this psychiatrist on the upper East Side for a few months. I thought I was going crazy and needed help. And it was all free because I was on Medicaid. For six months, I milked Medicaid dry. I had three teeth filled, got new glasses, had my ingrown toenail trimmed, and signed up as a patient of Dr. Lawrence Pendleton, the psychiatrist. Then they tightened up the rules and canceled my Medicaid card.

I figured no army would accept a physical and psychological wreck like me. But I'm not sure. I saw a friend of mine from the old neighborhood last week. He was home on leave. I met him on the street in front of Alexander's.

"All they want over there is warm bodies, Mike," he told me. "The VC don't care if you have asthma."

I don't think the psychiatrist would help me out much

if I asked him to write a letter to my draft board. When I told him that I no longer qualified for Medicaid, I hoped he would offer to see me for free, or at something less than his fifty-dollar-an-hour fee.

"I can't afford fifty bucks a week, Doctor," I told him. "That's just about what I get from my stipend."

"What do you plan on doing, then, Mr. Carolan?"

"I'm not sure," I said. "I was hoping maybe you'd consider seeing me for a smaller fee or something."

"I couldn't do that," he said. "Actually, I think if you had to pay for treatment, it might be a good indication of your motivation, your commitment to this process."

"But, Doctor, your fee would use up my entire stipend."

Dr. Pendleton sighed. "Mr. Carolan," he said, "many of my patients work hard to make enough money to pay for their sessions. You want something for nothing." I glared at him. "Why don't you get a job driving a cab?" he said.

"Doctor, I have too much school work to get a job. And getting a job would violate the terms of my fellowship. Besides, I can't drive."

"Well, Mr. Carolan, why don't you quit school, learn to drive, and get a job as a cabbie?" he said impatiently. I felt like I was back in grammar school.

"You mean you want me to drop out of school and get a job just so I can afford to see you?"

"If you think it's important enough."

I certainly didn't think it was important enough. Sure, I'm going to give up a very congenial arrangement that also keeps me and the Viet Cong on friendly terms just so I can lie on this guy's couch and read him my dreams.

Mr. King has the right approach to doctors.

Today is the first day of the 1970s. Last night was the night the 60s ended. "The Night the 60s Ended"—I think of last night in quotation marks. It was no big deal—just a small dinner party for five at my friend Rusty's place. He lives a few blocks down Fordham Road, in a high rise building across from Lamb's bookstore. You can see the Third Avenue El from the terrace off his living room.

Rusty is one of those obsessive types. As soon as you put out a cigarette, he cleans the ashtray. I can't stand that. You can never relax around that kind of person. I accuse him of being anal retentive. He admits it.

Rusty and I are alike in many ways. He's twenty-five (two years older than me), six foot two (one inch taller), and Irish-American (me too). His hair is falling out faster than mine. He combs it meticulously to cover the thin spots. We are both graduate students.

His tastes are much more highbrow than mine. Opera is more important to him than sex. Personally, if I never heard another opera, I think I would survive. I tried to get into it in college, but no dice. There's too much Art for me in opera. I think it obscures things. Christine says she can take it or leave it.

Rusty says Christine and I look alike. He says it with an air of superiority that really annoys me. He makes you feel like you don't have enough imagination to look different. Not that I agree with him. Like me, Christine is fair-skinned, wears glasses, and parts her hair down the middle. But that's it. Our noses are different. So are our lips and eyes. And I'm much taller.

Rusty and I argue frequently about Bob Dylan. Naturally, he hates Dylan. "Some of the songs are okay," he says, "but the man's voice—ugh! It sounds like an animal being tortured."

"What you don't see, Rusty," I patiently explained, "is that Dylan has liberated the human voice. Now people are allowed to sound like real human beings when they sing, instead of sounding like those ridiculous Carusos you opera buffs are so fond of."

"I hate the term 'opera buff,' " he says. "Please don't call me that. And if Dylan's singing is liberation, I'll take slavery any day."

Christine likes Dylan, thank God. We have all his l.p.'s and listen to them more than to anything else. I tell her to get a little high first, it will make the music invade your soul. But she rarely does. Christine is an old-fashioned girl.

She says pot freaks her out. She turned on last February when we went with some friends to the Academy of Music to see a Dylan film called "Eat the Document." It was originally made for t.v., but never got past the censors. There were only two shows. A long line appeared in front of the theater. We had to stand out in freezing rain and sleet for over an hour to get in. A.J. Weberman showed up. He's a real case. He handed out leaflets accusing Dylan of all kinds of fascist activity.

Once we got inside the theater the lights went down, one of my friends lit up a joint and passed it around. I was nervous, but smoked some anyway. It surprised me when Christine took a few drags. She became very sad. Halfway through the movie she said she felt sick. She went to the bathroom and returned in about ten minutes, looking drained. For the rest of the night, she acted kind of strange. I'm just as glad she doesn't usually smoke.

"Eat the Document" was weird. Somebody told me Dylan was doing a lot of speed while the film was being shot.

"That's the trouble with Mr. Dylan and Company," Rusty said last night after dinner. "Your mind has to be eaten away by drugs before any of it makes any sense."

"Drugs!" I said. "What a great idea! Let's do some drugs." I wasn't in the mood to argue with him. New Year's Eve—you're supposed to have a good time.

Then this guy named Greg Winter—a friend of Rusty's from his high school days—handed me a joint and said, "Here, smoke this."

Right off the bat, this guy had given me the creeps. All he did during dinner was smile. Without showing his teeth. He didn't talk. He had a cane hooked onto the back of his chair.

"What's the cane for?" I asked him.

"Greg was hurt in Vietnam," Rusty said.

"Sorry, man," I said.

"That's okay, brother," Greg said. "You weren't the one who shot me now, were you?" I laughed nervously. Greg laughed right at me.

"This dope?" I asked when he passed me the joint.

"No, man. It's red pubic hair. I grew it myself."

Christine told me afterwards that Greg scared her right away. She said he was watching me all through dinner. She was suspicious of him. She felt from the way he was observing me that he had something up his sleeve.

I took the joint from him and did some deep tokes on it.

"Funny taste," I said. Greg smiled at me. I passed the joint back to him, but he declined. "I'm there already, man," he said. Christine took a dainty puff on it and coughed immediately. Rusty never smokes. He doesn't believe in drugs. Plus, he thinks any kind of smoking contributes to hair loss. The only other person at the party, a fellow student of mine and Rusty's named Maureen Collins, is also a nonbeliever. "Wine's my drug," she says. "Can't cut loose without your juice?" I say to her. Maureen has a cheeky Irish face, red as an apple. "That's right, Michael," she says.

I smoked some more of the joint.

"What was it like over there, in Vietnam?" Christine asked Greg.

"Let's let Saigons be bygones," he said.

Rusty turned on the t.v. to watch Guy Lombardo ring out the old. I tried to focus on the screen, but my vision wouldn't come together and a strange feeling shot up my legs. I started to feel paralyzed. Christine noticed the change in me.

"What's wrong?" she said.

"Something. I don't know."

Guy Lombardo was playing "Auld Lang Syne." Greg watched me closely. I realized too late I was part of an experiment.

I made it to the bathroom. My legs felt like lead. I threw up. I lost control of my bowels. My eyes were watering. I was afraid.

Rusty and Christine helped me out of the bathroom. They guided me into Rusty's bedroom and made me lie down. Christine was upset and furious.

"What was in that joint?" I could hear her asking Greg.

"Hey, take it easy, sister," he said. "Just a little angel dust. It won't hurt him."

"Won't hurt him!" Christine yelled. "What kind of maniac are you, tricking people like that?"

"He'll be okay," Greg said. "He's a tough guy, right?"

Christine got sick too, but not as violently as me. Maureen left right after they put me in the bedroom.

Rusty, Greg, and Christine came into the bedroom to check up on me. I was lying on my back with my hands folded on my belly, my eyes closed. I thought I was dead. This was my wake. The three of them stood around the bed.

"Doesn't he look grand?" I said in a Irish brogue. "So lifelike. He looks better than he did when he was alive, God rest his soul." Everything seemed very funny. "And he had his whole life ahead of him," I continued. "Such a shame. Cut down in his prime."

Greg laughed. I opened my eyes. Christine looked like she was in shock. Rusty looked worried.

I fell asleep. Rusty says I was out for almost two hours. When I woke up, Greg was gone. Christine was sleeping on the couch in the living room. Rusty was reading *Love's*

Body in the kitchen. All evidence of the dinner party had been cleaned up. I was grateful. The mere sight of leftover lasagna would have made me sick again. I asked Rusty for a glass of water.

"How are you feeling?"

"Wiped out." I woke up Christine. "I'm back from the dead," I said.

"I was really scared." she said.

"It's over now," I said. "Happy New Year."

"That was a terrible thing for that guy to do."

"Sure was," I said. "Let's go home."

"Let me get myself together first," she said. She picked up her shoes and pocketbook and headed for the bathroom. Rusty came into the living room.

"You got some real entertaining friends," I said.

"Michael, I'm sorry. I really am. I asked him to leave. I guess the war scrambled his brains."

I love the way Christine cares about me. She wants to be an artist. She seems very fragile to me sometimes. But I know she has a lot of strength. We married ourselves on the street last fall. We stopped on the corner of 5th Avenue and 34th Street, held hands, and declared ourselves married.

Christine worries that maybe our "marriage" won't last. I tell her the Irish have a saying: the hottest love is the soonest cold. "So, be cool," I say.

▼

FLAMES

AT FOUR A.M. APRIL was awakened by cries of "fire!" Still half asleep and groggy, she threw on her bathrobe and opened the door. Richie was in the hallway, naked. "Fire," he yelled when he saw her, "my room's on fire." He was in a panic. April never woke up easily or quickly. She watched Richie run into the bathroom on the landing outside her room. Naked, he seemed thinner to her than she thought he would. His body looked milky in the dim light of the landing. The whole scene had a dreamlike feel to her.

He came running out of the bathroom with a plastic bucket filled with water. April still hadn't moved. "April c'mon, help. There's a fire in my room." She could smell the fire. Smoke curled down the stairway that led to Richie's attic. He rushed up the stairs with the bucket of water.

April had been dreaming about Richie before his shouts woke her up. She had started dreaming about him months ago, right after she moved into the house. In her dreams, the two of them drive around all night in an enormous old car looking for a store that sells Hawaiian shirts. Or they tear through the streets of the city, pursued by scores of policemen.

April was starting to come out of her haze of sleep. She ran into the bathroom, looked around desperately for something to put water in, but couldn't find anything. Finally, she picked up the cat litter box, dumped its contents down the toilet, filled it with water, and raced out of the bathroom. By now Richie was back down on the landing, still naked, and coughing almost uncontrollably. His eyes were watering. "Forget it," he said to her, "it's gone too far." He sounded as though he were crying. April stood their holding the cat box. "I'll call the fire department," he said. He ran off to the phone in the bedroom next to hers, normally occupied by their vacationing housemates Frank and Betsi.

April decided to throw the water on the fire. She ran up the narrow stairs to the attic, trying to keep the water from spilling. At the top of the stairs, she flung the water into the room. She could see it was hopeless. The whole room seemed in flames. The sight of Richie's few furnishings, and his drawings and paintings, burning up so rapidly terrified her. She had never been near a real fire before.

By the time she got back down to the second-floor landing she could hear the sirens and horns of the firetrucks. Richie had put on a pair of blue jeans and a shirt belonging to Frank.

"Why did you go up there?" he asked. "I told you it was too late." April's lungs hurt from the smoke she inhaled during her brief encounter with the fire. She was trying to keep from crying. "I don't know," she said. "I thought I could do something." He put his arms around her. "Are you okay?" he asked. Before she could say anything, they heard glass shattering downstairs. They ran down in time to open the door for the firemen. The firemen had broken some of the door's glass panels and were all set to chop the door down with their axes.

There were six firemen. They burst into the house dragging a giant hose. They brushed Richie and April aside impatiently and hurdled up the stairs, lugging the hose up with them. They heard more glass shatter at the back door and again got to the door and unlocked it a moment before the axes would have smashed it to pieces. Four more firemen were at the back. April could sense that the firemen were annoyed at having been stopped from breaking down the doors.

She went into the kitchen and wrapped her arms around herself. Richie joined her and brushed the hair from her face. "I'm sorry," she said. "All your stuff is destroyed."

"No, don't worry," he said. "I left most of my work at my old studio. I just had a few new pieces here. And I wasn't too crazy about them. Maybe it's a message from God that he doesn't like my new work."

"Don't say that," she said. "I loved the ones you showed me."

She liked Richie's energy, his sense of purpose. Most of the men she went out with were ambitious, but it was not spiritual ambition. They wanted to make a lot of money, or be the boss at their jobs. Richie, she thought, wanted to be great.

A few weeks ago he quoted her a line he had read by a painter he admired: "When you're young, you want to be someone. When you're older, you want to do something." He was only twenty-seven, two years older than her, but she could tell he had reached a certain level of maturity with his work. Sometimes she felt she didn't understand his paintings. But she could feel their depth. She was not one of those people who think, "I could do that if I wanted to." She had seen only a few of his paintings, but she knew there was skill, maybe even genius, in the way the colors exploded over the horizon that cut across the middle of his canvases. He had a part-time job in the Senate mailroom. The attic was his bedroom and studio, and he was always talking about moving to New York and making it in the art world.

The firemen were done in under ten minutes. They told Richie and April that the damage wasn't extensive. The contents of the room were destroyed, but the structure was fine. They threw most of Richie's smoldering things out the window and onto the tiny front yard. Frank and Betsi's room, beneath the attic, was water damaged, but not too badly. It was a small fire.

"I think those guys were a little disappointed," Richie joked after the firemen had left. "I mean, I think they were hoping for The Towering Inferno."

April went back up to her room to change out of her bathrobe and put on some regular clothes. She was still coughing. The entire house stank of smoke and fire. Richie found some pieces of plywood in the basement and nailed them over the spaces in the doors where the glass had been. April joined him later in the kitchen.

"Frank and Betsi will be shocked," she said.

"Not to mention the landlord."

"Well, he must be covered for fire."

"He better be."

"What happened anyway?" April asked.

"The cat knocked over a candle while I was sleeping."

April worked as a researcher for WTTG, way up Wisconsin Avenue. Someday she wanted to be a deejay. For now, she was glad not to be a waitress. She hated waiting on people. She knew older women who never got out of the waitress trap, and she'd made up her mind that that wouldn't happen to her.

She absorbed other people's moods. It was a relief to her that Richie was so casual about the fire. It helped keep her calm. Her own impulse was to go to pieces, have a good cry.

She could feel the pressure of her emotions swelling inside her and fought to keep them under control. But now that the crisis was over and the fire out, she began to cry a little.

Richie didn't say anything. But again he put his arms around her. He could feel her body shudder. She shook herself and laughed. He grabbed a paper towel and handed it to her. She blew her nose and patted the tears on her face.

"I'm sorry," she said. "I think the fire just hit me. We could have been killed. I'm glad you woke up in time."

"It was my first fire. I hope my last."

"Frank's pants are too big. They look silly on you." As soon as she said this, she blushed, feeling as though she had noticed something intimate. She flashed again on Richie's naked, milky body.

"Let's get out of here," he said. "The smoke is too much."

"Where will we go? It's five a.m."

"Do you have any money?" he asked. "My cash went up in smoke."

"I have some."

"How much?"

"A few hundred dollars."

"Amazing," Richie said. "Give it to me. I'll pay you back as soon as I can get to the bank."

They waited for a cab on Columbia Road. Day was breaking, but they were alone on the street.

"I love it when the city is like this. So peaceful and quiet," he said.

"Like a ghost town. It's hard to believe the rat race will be in full swing in a few hours."

"Life's rich tapestry," he said.

The cab driver told them he was on his way home, but would drop them off at the hotel first. Richie took her hand in the back set of the cab.

"I don't know about this," April said. "I never stayed in a hotel before." She felt nervous.

"You'll love it," he said. "Don't worry. Nothing has to happen. I mean, with you and me."

"It's okay," she said. "Something can happen."

"I have to see a driver's license or a credit card. Some kind of i.d.," the clerk at the hotel told them. The clerk clearly disapproved of their disheveled appearance.

"We have cash in hand. What do you need i.d. for?" Richie asked.

"I'm sorry, sir. It's house policy." Richie asked to speak to the manager. After a few minutes, an older man appeared, trying to shake himself awake. April thought Richie handled him deftly. Richie explained in an authoritative, dignified way that they had just survived a fire, their identification was destroyed, and he and his wife simply needed a decent place to stay for the rest of the day. The manager suspended the rules, accepted $130 for the room, and shuffled back to dreamland.

April was dazzled by their room. It contained the largest bed she had ever seen, a huge color TV, an assortment of liquor in tiny bottles, and several bottles of Cokes and club sodas in the refrigerator. Two little pieces of Godiva chocolate wrapped in gold paper awaited them on the dresser.

"You told him I was your wife."

"He never would have believed you were my mother."

Richie went into the bathroom to take a shower. April sat on the bed and carefully unwrapped one of the chocolates and ate it very slowly, listening to the roar of the shower. She tried to imagine Richie washing himself, but her mind was blank as she watched the sun come up over St. Matthew's Cathedral.

▼

CAPTIVITY

SHE DECIDED SHE would write him another letter. It would be sane, rational, with no passionate statements, no announcements concerning all the wonderful things she would do to him the next time they were alone. The letter would display her calm, her new approach. He wanted signs of emotional maturity from her. Yesterday he said, "Your obsessiveness is driving me crazy. You're controlling me." The letter would prove she was not that kind of person. She was independent, together, worthy of him.

She would bring the letter to him at work. Just hand it to him without saying anything and leave quickly. No scenes. He hated scenes, especially at the store and especially when he was behind the register. She had to change her clothes first. He didn't like the way she dressed. In the beginning, he thought she looked cute with her black cap, blue harem pants, tattered cowboy shirt, and a Winston sticking out of her mouth. "How's the waif?" he would ask. Now it got on his nerves. He told her she should buy some new clothes. "You look ridiculous," he said.

He called her "the detective." She was always trying to figure everything out. She knew his every move. He lived by routines. You could set your watch by when he bought the papers in the morning, or took his lunch break, or walked home at night. She could hunt him down like a bloodhound. He was flattered by her attention when it all started. But now she saw his panic. "I feel trapped," he said. "You never ease up." These days when she tracked him down, she pretended it was a coincidence. She caught him last night at the Cafe Don on Columbia Road. He stopped in after work for a beer. She knew he'd be there. "I ran out of cigarettes," she told him. "I just came in to use the cigarette machine."

She looked for an outfit he would approve of. Her wardrobe was an eccentric collection of thrift store bargains—antique dresses that didn't fit right, once-stylish jackets with enormous shoulder pads that made her head look like it had sunk down into her collar bone. And beads, necklaces, pins, and assorted jewelry that, he said, made her look like a gypsy. "You're an attractive woman," he said. "Why do you want to look so outlandish?" She thanked God she was pretty. Her legs were too short, but she had wild blonde hair, a good figure, and a cute, upturned nose. "I love your nose," he said. "It's classic American."

She was the opposite of him. "Your life is a hymn to chaos," he once said to her. He told her she should eat and sleep regularly, and take better care of her body, and maybe she wouldn't feel so wound up all the time. She wanted to move in with him, but he said no. He liked to be left alone. He suggested that she take hot baths to calm down. He gave her Valium when things got really out of hand, like the time a black guy in Dupont Circle came on to her and she cursed at him and the guy slapped her in the face. He told her she should have ignored the guy, that it was her self-destructiveness coming out again. "You want to get hurt," he told her. "You thrive on disaster."

She picked out her simplest clothes—a black wrap-around skirt and an army shirt. She knew he would be angry when she showed up at the store with another letter. It would be the second letter today. But at least she hadn't phoned him yet. Lately he had begged her to back off. "Look, this is crazy," he said. "You write me three or four letters a day sometimes, not to mention phone calls. I want a break. Please just give me a break."

He was tall and intelligent. She loved his eyes and his sense of humor. Before things got really terrible, he made her laugh all the time. He took her to movies and Chinese restaurants. She felt safe with him. He encouraged her to write and to paint. "You're a natural," he said. His looks were unconventional, but she thought he was beautiful. She told him he looked like a Greek statue.

She called the store. When she heard his voice, she hung up. She wanted to make sure he hadn't gone home sick. He complained all the time that he didn't feel well. He had a sensitive stomach and sinus trouble. She hoped he hadn't guessed it was her calling. That drove him crazy. "Don't play those games with me," he warned.

Last night was terrible. After they left the Cafe Don, they had a awful argument at his apartment. When she brought the first letter to him this morning, an hour after he had punched in, he looked at her in disbelief. The letter said how much she loved him. She loved his eyes and hair and his long delicate nose. She reminded him of good times they had shared. She described in detail how she would make love to him next. He scowled at her. "I can't read this now," he said. "I'm too busy." He folded the envelope and stuck it in the back pocket of his jeans.

She made a cup of coffee and sat by her living room window, looking down at the traffic on Florida Avenue.

D.C. was worse than Tulsa, her hometown. He was the only thing that kept her here. She took a deep drag on her cigarette. She could not accept last night. She could not handle what he had said to her. By now, he had probably read her first letter. She came on too strong. She had to make him feel that she didn't need him so much. The second letter had to get through to him.

She remembered how his face had sunk when she walked into the Cafe Don and he saw her. He sat in a booth in the back, both hands around a stein of beer, talking with a friend from work. The friend left after she joined them in the booth. She tried to convince him that she wasn't out looking for him, it was just a coincidence. She pleaded with him to believe her. He took off his glasses and rubbed his face. "Okay, okay," he said. She grabbed his hands and said that she knew he wanted more freedom, she was aware of that, she wasn't stupid. She said she knew she couldn't push him too far. Without his glasses, his face had a blank look. She thought he looked like a bird with that dumb look in his eyes. She knew he was trying to tune her out. Nothing drove her more crazy than that. She started shaking his hands. His beer almost spilled over. He put his glasses back on. She told him he had to believe her. Other people in the restaurant became aware of them. He couldn't stand that. Nothing made him more tense than arguments in public. "Let's get out of here," he said very calmly. "We'll talk about it at home." He didn't wait for his check. He left four dollars on the table, got up and put on his pea coat.

Her mother and father used to fight all the time. She felt incredibly close to her mother. At fifty-three, her mother still looked beautiful. Her father was an old man, almost twenty years older than her mother. They lived in Florida now. She wanted to visit them, but hadn't in over two years. She couldn't stand to be around her father. The old man hated her. He blamed her for his miserable marriage.

She knew they got married because her mother was pregnant. After she was born, her mother lost all affection for
her father. He was old and in the way. When she was
fourteen, her father tried to punish her for coming home
late from a dance. She laughed at him. That was the last
time the two of them paid any attention to each other.

She couldn't find the right beginning for the letter. She
wanted it to sound poised and coherent. It wouldn't be like
her other letters, full of passion and sincerity, like the letter
she gave him this morning. He told her recently that he
was sick of her "little girl act." He said that he was not the
beginning and end of the world, that she would have to try
to make herself happy. She couldn't leave it all up to him.
He wouldn't talk to her once they left the Cafe Don last
night and headed home. His anger scared her. She kept
trying to pull him closer to her and he kept creating more
and more distance. Back at his apartment, she started crying. He shook his head in frustration. It was her turn to get
mad. She asked him just who he thought he was—God?
She gave him everything—her love, her body, all kinds of
presents, exotic pastries. She took care of him when he was
sick. She'd do anything for him. But he didn't care. He was
so high and mighty.
He sat behind his desk and didn't say anything. She knew
he was nervous. She stood in the middle of his living room
screaming at him and crying. She said he was just using her,
he was selfish and arrogant. He said, "C'mon, keep it down.
The whole world doesn't have to hear us." He once told
her that he never saw his parents argue. They seemed to be
in love through over thirty years of marriage. When his
mother died, his father lost interest in life. His upbringing,
he said, left him with a terror of emotional violence.
She told him she didn't care who heard them, she was
going crazy. He got up from his desk and came towards

her to calm her down. Before he could put his arms around her and smooth things over, she pushed him with all her might. He almost fell over. Before he had time to regain his balance, she pushed him again and he fell to the floor.

She started to write. "Baby, I'm sorry, I'm sorry, I'm sorry. Please believe me. It'll never happen again. I promise." She tore the paper up and threw the scraps on the floor. Her sloppiness irritated him. Sometimes when she was upset, she flicked her ashes on the floor. He would hit the ceiling. "Will you please use the ash tray?" he'd say.

The tone had to be right. She was scared. She wanted to pour herself out on the page, tangle him up in a net of raw emotion. But she knew that approach wouldn't work this time.

Her face was swollen from crying. He blew up last night after she pushed him. She thought maybe some line had finally been crossed. He told her yesterday after the fight, "Don't bother with the letters. I'm not going to read them anymore. I'll tear them up. Don't waste your time." Maybe he hadn't even read her first letter this morning.

She tried again. "I know how you must feel about me," she wrote. "And you're right. I don't know what I can say to make things better again." She crumpled up the paper and threw it across the room. The cat scrambled after it and knocked it back under the table between her bare feet. She tried to think up another approach. After their last big fight two and a half weeks ago, he said to her, "You've tricked me back into staying with you once too often. You can't talk someone into loving you." She wished he were here right now and everything was okay between them.

When he got up off the floor last night, he didn't say a word. He sat down at his desk and she sat in the rocking chair. It seemed to her that hours passed before they talked again. He stared at a map of Paris hanging on the wall. He wouldn't look at her and the panic built up inside her. Then he said to her, "I don't love you. I wish we had never met." As soon as he started talking, she started saying no, no, no, I love you. He said, "Please get out of here."

She knew when she walked into the store this morning and gave him the first letter that he was still angry with her. That's when she decided that she had to write a different kind of letter, one that would really get through to him and convince him that they could work things out.

▼

ACTS OF RESISTANCE

AFTER ALMOST TWENTY years as a smoker, Willie had
given up cigarettes. During the day he pretended to be
going about his life normally, but inside all he could think
about were cigarettes. At night he had vivid dreams of
smoking. In his dreams he could feel the smoke filling up
his lungs again with a wonderful sense of relief.

"I'll never stick to this," he told Madeleine. "God meant
for me to be a smoker. My body chemistry is extremely
compatible with the activity of nicotine."

"That's ridiculous," she said. "Smoking is just an ugly
habit. I know it's been hard for you, baby, but you can do
it. It's already been a few weeks."

"Yeah, but look at all our friends. Michael stopped for
three months and went back. Martha stopped for almost
six months. I talked to my sister Rose last week. She gave
them up for six years and went back. Six years! I keep
thinking it's inevitable that I'll go back, so why bother
going through all this withdrawal."

"Lots of people stay off forever," Madeleine said.

"Think of that."

"God didn't mean for them to be smokers," Willie answered. Madeleine ignored him. Willie's flippancy sometimes got on her nerves.

"I can't tell you how nice it is for me that you don't smoke anymore. I hate cigarette smoke. And I used to worry so much about you. I don't want to outlive you."

"We weren't built to last," Willie said.

"You're doing so good with it, baby. I'm proud of you. You haven't been cranky at all. What day are you up to?" Willie removed the toothpick from his mouth for dramatic emphasis.

"This is Day Eighteen," he said solemnly.

* * *

On Day Nineteen, Willie got home at three a.m. from a job in Alexandria. Madeleine was sound asleep when he stumbled into the dark bedroom. Willie's lower back hurt since he gave up smoking. He also had sores in his mouth from chewing four packs of sugar-free gum in one hour on Day Seventeen.

He took off his clothes and dumped them on top of the dresser. He felt around for the flashlight, found it under a pile of dirty tee shirts and underwear, switched it on and headed towards the bathroom. All of a sudden, Madeleine bolted up and exclaimed, "I smoked the joint without the feathers!" At first Willie thought she was really awake. Then he realized she was still asleep. He went over to the bed and put his arms around her. "It's okay, kid," he said, "you're having a dream." Madeleine dreamed every night: horror stories, trips to heaven, hot pursuits, and biographical re-caps featuring everyone she had ever known. Willie didn't dream until he gave up cigarettes. Madeleine was still excited. "Don't be silly," she said, "you know what I mean—the feathers without the smoke." Willie laughed. Madeleine laughed too and shook her head. "I'm sleeping," she said, apologizing. "I'm going back to sleep."

"You're my all-time favorite," Willie said. He couldn't remember where he put the flashlight and tripped over the toolbox on the way to the bathroom.

* * *

One time in his sleep Willie woke up Madeleine in the middle of the night, gave her a hug, and whispered in her ear, "Keep on the sunny side." Madeleine told him that he talked in his sleep all the time. He even laughed in his sleep. Once he woke her from a deep sleep and said, "Wake me when we get there." Willie was amused by these tales of his sleeping self, but secretly felt alarm at this loss of control.

They were both fairly big people and took up a lot of room in bed. During their first year together, they fought all the time, frequently while asleep. Willie would pull the covers off Madeleine or Madeleine would spread out and force Willie onto a small corner of the mattress. Finally, Willie asked a friend to build them a queen-size platform bed to replace the old double brass bed that sagged in the middle. Now they each had plenty of territory in bed.

"I can't tell you what a great idea this bed was," Madeleine told him. "It changes everything."

"Stick with me, sweetheart," he said, "this ain't nothing."

"I'm serious," she said. "It was a stroke of genius."

"They don't call me the Imperfect Thirty-Two-Year-Old Master for nothing."

Willie missed the old brass bed. Some friends had given it to him years ago. His entire romantic life until Madeleine had been played out on that bed. He considered it holy, the altar of his past. He put up a notice on the bulletin board of the building where they lived and a tenant on the fourth floor bought the brass bed for a hundred and twenty five dollars. It made Willie vaguely uncomfortable to know that his old bed was still close by and accumulating a new history.

* * *

In spite of his strict Irish-Catholic upbringing, Willie was no longer very religious. Madeleine disputed this. She felt that Willie was still far too Catholic. He treated Sunday morning breakfast as though it were High Mass. He would lift the soggy filter over the Chemex and chant make-believe Latin: summa agricola jambolaya. "Don't be blasphemous," Madeleine would say to him. He never let her make the coffee.

"I could make good coffee if I put my mind to it," she said. "It's just a mechanical act."

"It's a sacrament," Willie said.

On Sunday, Day Twenty of Willie's life as a non-smoker, they had an argument after Madeleine broke one of Willie's Chinese bowls. "Why can't you be more careful?" he snapped at her, and she exploded. "Oh, it's such a big deal, right?" she said sarcastically, "one of your precious little bowls." Willie never broke anything. Madeleine accused him of being "obsessed with control."

* * *

They almost never went to bed together. Nor did they wake up together. Madeleine had a nine-to-five proofreading job at an office near Connecticut and K. She profoundly resented her job. Madeleine was a free spirit. She was not one of those people who need a job to give their lives structure. She wanted to get up when she felt like it, take photographs all day if she were in the mood, and go to bed as late as she wanted. Willie felt guilty that Madeleine had to work.

"In the old days," he said, "a woman didn't have to work."

"We need the money, sweetheart," she said. "I

don't mind."

"You hate it," he said. "If you stayed with Eddie the law student, you'd be sitting pretty now."

"But it was you I wanted, not Eddie the law student."

Willie worked as engineer and chief assistant to the boss of Alligator Sound, a company that provided audio equipment and the people to run it. He worked concerts, bars, conventions, and festivals in the Washington area. Alligator also did some recording at its small studio in Bethesda. Willie's schedule was erratic. He was gone frequently at night and home during the day. There were weeks when Madeleine and Willie hardly saw each other.

For ten days after he gave up smoking, Willie had trouble sleeping. He'd sneak into bed at three or four in the morning, hoping not to wake up Madeleine, who was a very light sleeper, and lie there trying to relax. But his body felt like it was exploding with energy. He'd move around constantly, trying to find the right position in which to fall asleep. Madeleine would sooner or later half wake up, annoyed that he had disturbed her. "I have to get up for work. Can't you be still?" Willie went out on Day Eleven and bought a foam rubber mattress and took to sleeping on the living room floor.

"Baby, this is crazy," Madeleine told him. "We hardly see each other. And now we don't even sleep together."

"It'll pass," Willie said.

"C'mon, you know it's always going to be like this. Me sleeping, you out on the town. We never do anything together. We never take a vacation together."

"C'mon," he said, "we had Chinese food the day before yesterday."

"You know what I'm talking about." She was exasperated. "The only time we see each other is a few hours at night when we're both sleeping."

"We get along much better when we're asleep."

"Please don't joke, okay? We're talking about our life together."

"What do you want me to do? You want me to give up a job I love and work in an office?"

"Maybe you should think about it," Madeleine said. But she knew she couldn't ask him to give up something he loved and become part of the nine-to-five world just to share her misery. He'd only hate her for it eventually. And if she were in his position, she'd feel the same as he did.

He put his hand on her forehead and brushed back her thick black hair. "Listen, some day we'll have lots of money and we can do what we want. Take trips around the world. Buy a house with a swimming pool."

"That's never going to happen," she said, "and you know it. We're always going to be scrambling to get by." He continued to rub her forehead. She loved the way he touched her. When she first met him, she thought his touch would be nervous, skittery. He seemed like he had too much crazy electricity running through him. She remembered how surprised she was the first time he put his arms around her. He felt so strong and peaceful to her.

"Hey, be more optimistic," he said. "You have to look at the bright side of things."

"I feel trapped," she said. "All I do is go to work, come home and eat, force myself to stay up for a few hours, then go to bed again. I never see you. I never have time for my own work. It really gets to me after a while." Willie continued to soothe her.

"I know it's hard for you," he said. "But I think if we can stick it out and save some money, the sun's going to shine on us before too long. I got a lot of big ideas."

"I don't mean to lay all this on you," she said. "It's not your fault. I know you try. Maybe you're right. Maybe things will get better."

* * *

In his dream, Willie had a cigarette going in every ashtray. He smoked one after another. His friends all came over to hang around and smoke and help celebrate his return to the fold. Everyone was happy. Willie took an incredibly deep drag and let the smoke inflate his lungs.

In the morning, he was desperate for a cigarette.

"I dreamed about smoking all night," he told Madeleine. The alarm had gone off at eight and Madeleine was scurrying around the bedroom, trying to assemble an outfit she hadn't already worn to work that week. Then she realized it was Monday and she didn't have to worry about what she'd worn the day before. "Go back to sleep, honey," she said to Willie. "You didn't get to bed till four thirty."

"I can't sleep," he said. "I'm too wired. My skin hurts."

"Whatever," Madeleine said. She was getting impatient with Willie's martyrdom.

"This is my anniversary," Willie told her.

"What are you talking about?"

"Day Twenty One. Three weeks today."

"Congratulations," Madeleine said, squeezing into tight jeans from which she had removed the "Calvin Klein" label. She grabbed a blue workshirt with cowboy buttons and put it on.

"Is this too informal?"

"No. You look great," Willie said. "More beautiful than a dancing cigarette pack."

"Shut up," she said, giving him a kiss. "I've got to run."

"Pray for me," Willie said.

"You'll be fine. Don't give in to temptation." She gave him another kiss. "I'm going to be late again."

"Take a cab, my treat," Willie said.

"We can't afford it. Happy anniversary. A thousand kisses to you."

Willie got out of bed as soon as Madeleine left. He rolled a joint in the living room, smoked half of it, and went back to bed. He felt the pressure building immediately inside his head and started having difficulty swallowing. Good stuff, he thought, as he drifted back to sleep.

His dreams took him to Ireland and Canada. He sat with Madeleine inside a little cottage in Galway where his ninety-one year old aunt lived. She held their hands and asked them, "Are you enjoying life?" In Canada, he was given a pack of no-risk cigarettes, a new invention. Smoke as many as you want and they do no harm. Taste good, too. The phone in the living room woke him two hours later. He cursed it from the bedroom and waited for the ringing to stop. He never answered the phone when he thought it inconvenient.

Just as he was falling back asleep, the phone rang once and stopped. Willie waited. Their secret signal. It resumed ringing. "Hello," he said. He was annoyed that Madeleine would call so early.

"You don't sound too cheerful," Madeleine said.

"You shouldn't call me this early," Willie complained.

"Hey, it's almost afternoon," she said. "Don't be so grumpy."

"I just don't like to talk on the phone till I'm ready."

"That's not the kind of attitude that made America great," Madeleine kidded him. Willie didn't laugh. "Hey, c'mon," she said, "cheer up. This is your one and only."

"Okay. All right. What's up?" He was still annoyed. Madeleine resented him acting irritated. She was stuck in a stupid office on a Monday morning while he lounged around the apartment. Neither of them said a word. The silence lasted almost a full minute.

"This is ridiculous," Willie said. "Will you please tell me why you called?"

"Oh, right, it's my fault. I try to be nice and you act

rotten, but everything is my fault."

"Calm down," he said. "You don't have to make everything the end of the world. Let's not fight."

"I'm not looking for a fight. And I get a little tired of you always blaming me when this happens. Why is it always my fault?" Willie knew she was right and began to soften.

"It's not your fault. I'm sorry. Let's be friends."

"I'm sorry, too," Madeleine said. "I know you feel a lot of tension."

* * *

Everything began to taste great to Willie, especially sweets. In the afternoons, he took to visiting a nearby ice cream parlor for a cup of mocha chip with chocolate sprinkles. He was never interested in ice cream before. At the supermarket he stocked up on cookies and cake. Banana fudge loaf, Danish walnut ring, hazelnut cookies. He bought jams and cheeses, chocolate bars, peanut butter, and carob-coated raisins. By Day Twenty-Four, he had gained seven pounds.

He started to give Madeleine pet names based on food. He called her Sweet Potato, Peaches, Pudding, and Sugarfoot.

"I'm not sure I like all these food names," she told him. "Do you think I'm fat?"

"No, you're just right. Perfect."

"I think you think I'm too fat."

"Hey, forget it. You're a state-of-the-art girlfriend." Madeleine was beautiful. Willie thought she looked like Maria Schneider, Brando's co-star in "Last Tango in Paris." He called her "movie star" and told her she was the sexiest woman he ever knew. Madeleine was a shy girl from a small town in Massachusetts. After graduating seventh in the Clark University class of '73, Madeleine came to Washington to work on Capitol Hill in the office of a Boston Congressman. She discovered that she hated

politics and after fourteen months she abandoned her
career in government to become a photographer. Someday
she hoped to make a living taking pictures.

Willie migrated to Washington from his native New
York in the early '70s after dropping out of graduate school
(NYU) to help set up a draft counseling office in D.C.
When the anti-war movement disintegrated, he began a
succession of careers (including folk-singer, bartender,
mailman, and carpenter's helper) that ended when he
became "an audio engineer," as he described himself, with
Alligator Sound. He met Madeleine at a Ry Cooder concert
in Lisner Auditorium. She was the date of a musician
friend of his who introduced them during intermission.
When the musician excused himself "to check out the
plumbing," Willie zeroed in on Madeleine. "Run away
with me to my castle in New Jersey," he said abruptly and
Madeleine laughed.

They started going out together and, after three months,
Willie moved in with her. The first year was terrible. They
drove each other crazy. Willie's swaggering self-confidence
and old-fashioned attitudes about men and women clashed
with Madeleine's independent spirit. The scars of their
first year—taped cracks in the glass doors of the kitchen
cabinet, the shards of a broken ceramic bowl waiting to be
reglued, a dent in the wastepaper basket, a Pentax with a
broken lens—decorated Madeleine's comfortable, if slightly
run-down, one-bedroom apartment in Dupont Circle.
They broke up for good three different times.

* * *

Willie used to tell people he had a nose like a dog.
Everyone in his family had a great sense of smell. But now
he felt like a prize bloodhound. He was constantly on the
scent of one thing or another: foods, perfumes, body odors.
But his nose was most attuned to the delicious aroma of

cigarettes. Sometimes in the morning the sudden smell of a cigarette would fill the kitchen, as though a ghost were there with him enjoying a smoke. At first he thought these experiences were some kind of olfactory hallucinations. But eventually he figured that his nose must be picking up on smoke wafting up from the street, five stories below.

During the long course of his habit, Willie had smoked just about everything: pipes, cigars, every kind of cigarette. Filter, non-filter, kingsize, regular, longs, menthols, lows, and highs. He blew better smoke rings than anyone he knew, but could never master the French inhale. He wondered it he were fooling himself now with this attempt to break free. "You can't just give up smoking," he explained to Madeleine. "You have to give up cigarettes every fifteen or twenty minutes, every time you crave one. It's a process involving thousands of acts of resistance."

Madeleine told him about Dr. Lee, an acupuncturist in town who had allegedly eliminated the desire to smoke in many of his patients by placing a needle in a particular spot on their ear lobes. She also knew of a hypnotist who was rumored to have had great success in curing people of their addiction to nicotine. Willie pretended to be interested in all this, but deep down he believed that no voo doo could help him. Will power was the only answer.

* * *

His good friend Jack called him up. A year ago, much to Willie's amazement, Jack gave up his three-pack-a-day habit for five months. Willie thought Jack was really going to stay off the habit forever. Then he went back.

"I learned one thing when I gave them up," Jack said. on the phone.

"What was that?" Willie asked. He was desperate for help, advice, anything that would make it easier.

"The desire for a cigarette," Jack told him, "cannot be

satisfied by a cigarette."

Willie regarded Jack as a very wise, philosophical man. He sometimes referred to the accumulation of Jack's insights and attitudes as "Jack Buddhism." But this advice escaped him.

"That's real interesting, Jack," Willie said, "but I don't connect with it. I mean, my desire for a cigarette feels very much like it could be satisfied by a cigarette."

* * *

"Are we sleeping together tonight, or are you staying in the living room again?" Madeleine asked.

"I don't know, babe," Willie said. "I'll see how I feel when I get home from this job. I've lost the desire to sleep. I just lie there staring at the ceiling waiting for it to get light."

"It'll get better," Madeleine said. "It takes time for your body to adjust."

"I hope it gets better soon," he said. "I don't understand how all these millions of smokers give them up."

"I miss you," Madeleine said. "I want you back."

"I want to do it," he said. "I want control over my life."

* * *

Two years before, Willie stopped at the Childe Harold for a beer and discovered Madeleine sitting at a table with an old boyfriend. He said a frosty hello to them, decided to skip the beer, and went home. When Madeleine returned to the apartment, Willie unleashed his jealous rage.

"What were you doing with him?" he wanted to know.

"It was totally innocent," Madeleine told him. "And I don't like being interrogated by you." Willie lit up a cigarette. "Please don't smoke," she said. "I can't stand it."

"Are you kidding? We're talking about you out on the town with some jerk in a smoke-filled bar and all you can say is 'please don't smoke'?"

"I'll say whatever I want."

"You're just trying to evade the issue."

"I don't have to listen to your nonsense. This is my place."

"You can have it. I'm leaving."

That was the third, and last, time they broke up. They met on the street six weeks later, had a friendly talk over a cup of coffee at Kramer's, and started seeing each other again.

"The men out there are horrible," Madeleine told him. "They all want to be big shots and run the world. And they're not as cute as you."

"So, I'm the least of many evils?"

"You're great. I miss your sense of humor and the way you hug me. And your various other talents, if you know what I mean," she said, raising her right eyebrow.

"I want you back," Willie said. "I miss you like crazy. Listen, no more fights, okay? We both have to learn how to swallow our pride. I'll try if you will."

"I don't want to fight any more. Life is too short."

"I'll be better. I promise. I'll do my exercises. I won't eat junk food. I'll try to spend more time with you. I'll even give up smoking."

"I'll stay on my side of the bed," she said.

"It's a deal."

* * *

It was three a.m. Day Twenty-Eight, Willie's four-week anniversary. He sat at his desk in the living room trying to read a few pages of the newspaper, which he hadn't had time to do earlier. He had just got back from a job in the country, a benefit concert featuring four old-time string bands, at which everything went wrong. Connections blew out, cords went dead, feedback more than music filled the hall.

His eyes were too sore and tired to read. His body felt worn down. He tried these days to avoid climbing into bed until he was exhausted, to lessen the risk of insomnia. He sniffed the tips of the fingers of his right hand and realized that the smell of tobacco was becoming more and more faint. In the ashtray on his desk was a half-smoked Marlboro left there the day before by his friend Jack. Willie lit it up, inhaled deeply until, before he knew it, he had smoked the butt right down to the filter. It felt great. Like a fish thrown back into the water, he thought. He washed his hands in the kitchen and rinsed his mouth out with orange juice. He knew Madeleine would be upset if she smelled cigarettes on him when he went to bed.

▼

THE AGE OF TRANSITION

JANET ROSS WANTED to be an actress. She had all the right things going for her. Beauty, big liquid eyes, freckles, a nice figure. She radiated intelligence and ambition. She thrived on hard work. She could sing like the lark in the morning. Her repertoire included everything from rock 'n' roll to folk, jazz, standards, and show tunes. She knew only a few chords on the guitar, but could re-tune it Joni Mitchell style and sound better than Joni Mitchell. Once she started tap dancing in Willie's apartment when he put on a record of Bill "Bojangles" Robinson singing "Doin' the New Low Down." Willie was impressed. When he was a tee-used to do mock-tap dancing on his stoop in the Bronx with some of his friends. They were usually drunk. When Janet started tap dancing in his apartment, Willie knew it was the genuine article. But she made a tremendous racket on his wood floor and he asked her to stop.

"That black girl downstairs will be up here in a minute with her dog," he said. Janet didn't say anything. She smiled at him. She smiled all the time. It was an incredibly winning smile, suitable for magazine covers, cigarette ads, and Hollywood stardom. It was pure magnetism. Willie had no defenses against it.

Janet stopped dancing. Willie suggested they catch Roy Bookbinder's last set at the Childe Harold. Bookbinder was a blues revivalist, a young white man who dressed in '30s-style clothes and played a wicked guitar. They arrived and found a small table in the back just as Bookbinder was finishing his third set. Bookbinder ended the last song of the set with an elaborate run on the guitar. But then he added a variation to the riff and gave it a double ending. The audience was about to applaud when he broke into yet another ornate variation on the run. He kept it up for about ten minutes, a symphony of endings. The audience was dazzled. No one could tell if this would be the final tag, and after a while the people in the club just settled back and ooed every now and then at a particularly stunning variant. When he finally stopped, the people in the audience felt like they had shared in some secret joke on music.

When Bookbinder finished, the room cleared out. There were only about eight people left for the last set.

Janet said they should move up front. Willie knew he couldn't make much of a case for staying where they were, so he agreed. He would have preferred to stay where they were. He wanted to be close to the music, but alone with her. But he knew she wanted to be right up there, on top of things. When they went to the movies, she always wanted to sit in the front row. This, he thought, was insane. It gave him a headache.

They moved up front. Bookbinder got back on the little stage for the last set. It was very intimate. He sang a few songs and asked for some requests.

Willie usually kept a low profile in this kind of situation, but the intimacy inspired him to call out "Never Cried 'Til My Baby Got on the Train." That was Willie's favorite cut from his only Bookbinder album.

Bookbinder pushed back his old fedora, twirled the end of his long mustache, and said, "Yeah, that's a good one," and started playing. Willie felt good. Just an hour or so earlier he had played that cut for Janet and she loved it. Now, as if by magic, he had the man himself singing it for her. When he played the record at his place, Willie told Janet to listen for his favorite verse:

> *Tell you what the mean old train will do*
> *It'll take away your baby*
> *And blow the smoke at you*

"I don't know," he told her, "that line really gets to me."

Bookbinder's live version was much longer than the one on the record. But he left out Willie's favorite verse.

"He left out my verse," Willie said. He felt disappointed and personally responsible.

"That's all right," Janet said.

Then Bookbinder started playing an old shuffle on the guitar and Janet really got into it. She began to tap dance sitting down. Without the restriction of being in his apartment, she really let go with her feet. She was attracting more attention than Bookbinder, her shoes clacking noisily on the floor. The few people in the audience looked at her. Bookbinder glanced down with godlike indifference from the stage. But Willie could tell he was annoyed. Janet was stealing the scene.

Willie was embarrassed. If he had been tap dancing like that, somebody probably would have told him to shut up. But no one would ever bother Janet. That smile was like the Gardol Protective Shield. It was the boyfriends who got in trouble.

"These beautiful ladies, you got to watch out," he told his friend Jack Harte. "They can get you in some real trouble if they want."

Janet was a descendant of Betsy Ross. She could trace her family line right back to The Mayflower and was entitled to join the D.A.R. if she chose to.

"The big ship in my family history is the Staten Island Ferry," Willie told her. She laughed. "And I'm entitled to join the A.O.H. if I want."

"What's the A.O.H.?" she asked.

"What's the A.O.H.?" He pretended to be amazed at her ignorance.

"Never heard of it," she said.

"It happens to be the Ancient Order of Hibernians," he said. "There's a rumor that I'm descended from some very royal ancient Hibernians."

"Yeah? Who started the rumor?" she asked.

"I don't know," he said. "Who created the universe?"

"Not the Irish, that's for sure," she said.

"Not the old bags in the D.A.R. either," he said.

"Don't worry. I'm not joining."

"That's a load off my mind," he said. "Think of what Joan Baez might do if she heard I was involved with someone in the D.A.R."

"You good friends with Joan Baez?" Janet asked.

"No, but I hear she's hot to meet me."

"Another rumor?"

"More like a murmur," he said.

Janet was an All-American girl. The first time he asked her if she wanted to stay over, she said, "I wasn't sure if you were interested in girls."

"I'm interested in you," he said.

Willie first met Janet through his friend Christopher Early. That was three years before Willie and Janet became lovers. Back then, his friend was going through a major change of life. At the age of thirty, Christopher left eight years of marriage and fatherhood for a life of freedom and promiscuity. Monogamy had built up in him an enormous appetite for sex. For a year and a half, Christopher experimented with his sexuality with an enthusiasm that was heroic, selfish, crazy, and inspirational. He found himself attracted not just to people, but occasionally to arms, faces, eyes, and other parts of the body, with an indifference to the total picture that Willie sometimes found startling.

At the same time as Christopher's change, Willie was himself breaking out of his past. He had been involved with a woman named Marianne for five years. But eventually the pressure he felt inside to explore his stranger side became too great and he and Marianne split up.

Christopher and Willie responded to their new freedom with the spirit of lifers who are granted an unexpected pardon and given a million dollars each. They whizzed around in Christopher's Toyota to countless bars, parties, and dances in search of instant love and exotic sex. They survived off unemployment checks, grants, part-time work, and the generosity of others. Their lives had opened up to a range of possibilities that they had only fantasized about in the past.

Christopher was the undisputed champ. He was handsome and intelligent and managed to preserve inside him an adolescent innocence that was often irresistible. He had tremendous, contagious energy. He claimed enviable sexual endurance. He could dance all night. He could eat twice as much as anyone else.

Janet and Christopher had a brief affair during this time. For about two weeks, Christopher seemed to be in love with Janet. But she was a difficult woman to get close to. She was capable of turning off other people with little effort.

"I can't figure her out," Christopher had told Willie. "I guess she's just real spaced out." Very quickly, her remoteness became more than Christopher was willing to put up with. In those days, he was drawn to uncomplicated pleasures with a variety of people. Janet did not fit into his plans and they stopped sleeping together.

Willie had always thought that Janet was attractive. But he never felt inspired to try to start anything with her. She was a little too beautiful. After Christopher moved to New York in search of the Big Time, Willie lost touch with Janet. She became a peripheral figure from the past. And it wasn't even his past—she was much more a part of Christopher's history.

By the time he left for New York, Christopher's appetite for sex had been transformed into an appetite for success. He settled down with a Latino woman named Mémé in a chic apartment in Little Italy. There he waited to be touched by fame.

Willie missed Christopher and New York. He made frequent trips to his hometown to visit his old friend. He felt comfortable and valued at Christopher's place. Mémé liked him and always made him feel welcome.

In January, almost a year after Christopher had left D.C., Willie paid a surprise visit and found that Janet was crashing there for a few days. She was in town to visit friends and pick up some information on acting schools in Manhattan. Mémé didn't seem to mind putting up Janet. Willie figured Mémé understood that Christopher and Janet had had only a minor affair. Or maybe Mémé didn't know anything about it.

Janet made almost no impression on Willie during that visit. He was too distracted by his life back home. Like many people in show business, Janet was full of good cheer and acted overjoyed to see him. She gave him a big hug and kiss when he arrived at Christopher's.

"Willie! Oh, it's so good to see you," she said. "It must be a year or two since we've seen each other!"

Christopher told him when they were alone that all sorts of men were in hot pursuit of Janet. She had been there only three or four days, but several hopefuls had already picked up the scent. It seemed to Willie that Janet found the attentions of men about as interesting as the weather. He doubted that she put out for any of those poor suitors who wanted her so badly. One poet, who lived down the block, hung around Christopher's place every day. He was a good-looking and talented man, but Janet treated him off-handedly and he seemed miserable and defeated.

When it came time for bed the night Willie arrived, Christopher pulled a mattress out of his huge closet. He got out some sheets and a blanket and two pillows.

"I hope you two don't mind sharing the mattress," he said to Willie and Janet.

"Just as long as she doesn't try anything funny," Willie said. Janet laughed, but her look suggested she was preparing to fend off yet another man. At this she was an expert and felt very confident. That she had no choice but to sleep with him only made her job more challenging.

But Willie was not thinking the thoughts Janet suspected of him. He was annoyed that he didn't get the mattress to himself as he usually did when he crashed at Christopher's.

Janet disappeared into the bathroom and came back out wearing a white nightgown that covered her body from her neck to her ankles. It dawned on Willie that she probably thought he would try to make some moves with her. He felt a secret satisfaction in knowing that the last thing on his mind was making it with Janet. But it was a hollow satisfaction. He wished he too wanted her badly. His indifference only reminded him of how confused he felt about his life.

She scooted under the covers in a flash. He turned out the light and walked over to the mattress. Then he took off his shirt and bluejeans and got into bed wearing red briefs.

The two of them lay on their backs staring at the ceiling.

"You want to get high?" Willie asked. "I got this roach right here."

"No thanks," Janet said.

Willie had the roach and ash tray ready to go on the floor next to the mattress. She probably figures I'm trying to get her high to weaken her defenses, he thought. He laughed to himself. He always got high before falling asleep.

"Listen, you better smoke some of this," he said.

"Why?"

"It makes you blind and crazy."

Janet laughed and decided to take a few tokes on the roach after all. She liked her drugs even more than Willie.

"You know something?" he said.

"What?"

"I've always wanted to sleep with you. And here I am. So after you get famous I can say, 'Oh, sure—the famous movie star Janet Ross? Yeah, I've slept with her.' "

Janet laughed again. She relaxed more as she began to feel that he wasn't going to try anything. She was a little confused as she shifted gears. Maybe he's gay, she thought.

She probably thinks I'm a faggot, Willie thought.

"Well, goodnight, Janet," he said.

"Good night."

"Chew your food," he said.

"Okay, I will."

Janet got them a ride to Baltimore with the brother of a friend of hers and two of the brother's friends. Willie sat in the back with Janet, the three guys sat up front. Willie didn't like her hat. It was a beat-up gray fedora like his father used to wear. He thought it looked a little too cute. She talked about her plans for the future. She was joining the Drama Shop in Washington, a small experimental theater group. She hoped to land a few parts in some of the

Shop's upcoming productions. She figured she'd have to work some low-level job to survive. Last year she sold beads and jewelry on the corner of Connecticut and K, she told him. And she might do that again if she had to.

He looked at her and wondered how seriously she took herself.

The three guys dropped them off at the bus station in Baltimore.

"Time to ride the Hound," Willie said. They had about forty minutes to kill in the bus station. He started to feel that having her with him was a real drag. She attracted attention on two fronts: she was pretty, she was wearing that ridiculous hat. Willie wanted to be anonymous. He didn't want anything to do with the large assortment of creeps to be found at any bus station.

But she was okay. He learned fast that she had mastered the art of de-fusing all the wired, hungry men who were forever crossing her path. She just removed herself. She made them tiny and insignificant. They felt the invisibility she conferred on them and simply faded away. She did it with grace and good humor. No hostility was necessary.

And she did take herself seriously. Willie started taking her seriously too. He wasn't sure if he bought her whole trip—the dedicated actress, willing to work hard and stay beautiful during her climb to the top. But he didn't want to dismiss it in case it was true. The same with religion— Willie had been a devout little Irish Catholic boy who went from "fallen away Catholic" as a teenager to rabid, Church-hating atheist in college. The only thing he felt now was that he didn't know. Maybe it was all true, maybe it's all nonsense. So he took religion seriously, but didn't get involved with it.

On the bus from Baltimore, Janet told him how she had recently spent three months in the West Indies, living in a little hut on the beach. A photographer from *Playboy* took some pictures of her while she was living at the beach, but for some reason the magazine never ran them. Willie felt relieved he wasn't in love with her. Imagine how crazy it would be. Beautiful woman, very hot number, sought after by everyone. Potential Playmate of the Year. She also told him that a group of men broke into her hut and came very close to killing her, or at least raping her, but somehow she got herself out of it.

Willie could see easily how she could have done it. Her eyes were big and deep. She simply didn't allow people to hurt her or interfere with her. People were hypnotized by her eyes. There were five men, she said. She was nude and they held a razor to her throat. But nothing happened. She just eluded them, slipped out of their grasp, ran away. She set up some kind of emotional force-field that they couldn't get past, like her Gardol smile.

They got to D.C. after an hour on the bus. Janet lived near the station. A bad neighborhood. Willie was usually very sensitive in these situations, in spite of his own paranoia. But he didn't even want to offer her an escort to her place. He felt out of it, surprised to be back in D.C., not ready for it. He wished Christoper still lived here. Christoper made Willie feel accepting of his ambiguities.

"Well, good night," she said, looking at him with those big eyes, her freckled face full of expectancy.

"Yeah, good night," he said. "It was good to see you again."

"Good to see you too. That was a nice ride together."

Then all of a sudden he felt guilty. He didn't want to walk her home. He just wanted to get in a cab, zip home, and resume feeling sorry for himself in private. He forced himself to make the offer, feeling like a real phony.

"Listen, you need some company getting to your place?"

"No, it's just a couple of blocks away. I'll be fine," she said.

"You sure?"

"Positive," she said. She threw him a smile. Then they hugged each other. She still had the hat on. They were on the sidewalk, in front of the station. The street was crawling with winos and bus station lowlifes. There were a couple of cabs at the curb.

"I'll call you soon," he said.

"Okay."

"You sure you don't want me to walk you?"

"It's fine. I do it all the time."

"Okay. Well, see you."

"Take it easy." She headed off down the street. He stood and watched her for a minute, feeling terrible. Don't let her get mugged, God, he prayed. A beauty like that roaming around the city's hot spots of crime and iniquity. He got a cab and took off for home.

Four months later, in May, Willie threw a party for a friend of his who was moving to New York. Among all his friends in town, Willie remained the one and only native New Yorker. But lately it seemed like every few months another friend would decide to leave for the big time in the Big Apple. And once they moved, his friends acted like supreme Manhattanites, contemptuous of anyone who lived outside of the three or four hip enclaves in New York. These were people from places like Idaho, Ohio, and Bethesda, Maryland. Two weeks in New York and they acted like they were born and raised in Soho and had never seen the sun set outside of lower Manhattan.

His friend Christopher was the worst. He was from New Jersey and all his life New York was so near, yet so far away. When he was still in D.C., Christopher was infatuated with New York. It was like Disneyland to him. He wanted to move up there someday.

When Christopher finally did move up to the big city,

he began to change his attitudes. He started treating Willie like some visitor from the boondocks, a country cousin from the embarrassing locale of his recent past. Gone was the status Willie enjoyed as a New Yorker in Washington. Christoper even started suggesting that his native New Jersey was really more or less a part of New York (less, definitely less, Willie thought) and that the Bronx was some very distant kingdom of wild dogs and crazy Puerto Ricans that didn't really deserve to be counted as part of the city. This annoyed Willie immensely. He should get a job in Russia re-writing history, Willie thought.

So now this other friend was making the big move and Willie called up everybody he knew to invite them to the party. He decided to include Janet. He hadn't seen her since they parted company at the bus station that night. He still felt bad about not walking her home. He liked her and didn't want any bad feelings between them. In fact, since their bus ride, he had thought about Janet frequently. Her beauty and vitality stuck in his mind.

He remembered how strange she seemed to him. Willie was fond of believing that most beautiful American women in their mid-twenties had been crazed acid freaks in their late teens. So many of them seemed weird and spaced out to him. And always the beautiful ones. He imagined that sometime after their 200th acid trip they experienced an ineffable illumination that, if it could be paraphrased, told them to give up acid and go out into the world and eat health food, do yoga, smoke pot, and break hearts. And succeed. Show the world you can be just as hungry, as ambitious, as pushy, in your own feminine way, as men. But space out a lot too, the illumination directed, in homage to the deep insights from your acid past. It was a simple and sexist key to their behavior that Willie didn't really believe. Or he did believe but didn't really think was true.

Life is a constant struggle against pain, Willie thought, and drugs are one of our best weapons in the fight. But he would never do acid. He thought he would instantly freak out and never come back. They would put him in a little room with rubber walls and he'd sit there on the floor and drool into old age, a ghost of the smart and sane man he used to be.

But marijuana he loved. He smoked it every day. Years ago he started selling it to help supplement his income. Dealing pot scared him when he first started. It was less accepted back then and more dangerous. But he got off on the exotic role of drug dealer.

Now it was very routine for him. He'd pick up a few pounds, spread some newspapers on his living room floor, and dump the dope on the paper. He'd put the phone on the floor next to him—as well as an ash tray, a little postage scale, a box of baggies, and a roll of Scotch tape—and start bagging the dope.

For his parties, he rolled up about five fat joints beforehand so he could get everyone smashed right away. By the time Janet arrived at the party, most of the people there were very stoned.

She looked great, he thought. Her smile beamed out all over the room, like an Ultra-Brite commercial. Half the men in his apartment immediately gathered around her. She smiled graciously, but kept her distance. She was at least democratic, Willie thought.

Later, he walked into the bedroom, on his way to the john, and discovered Janet sitting on his bed talking to a guy Willie had invited to the party. They were waiting for the bathroom. The guy had his charm turned up so high, he was feeding back. That boy is going nowhere, Willie thought. Janet was friendly and tolerant, but she might as well have had a moat stocked with starving sharks around her. The bathroom emptied. Janet took her turn. The guy asked Willie who she was.

"She's a friend of mine. An actress," Willie said.

"What a dish," the guy said. "She available?"

"Forget it," Willie told him. "You might as well fly to London and try to run off with the Queen."

Willie didn't talk much to Janet all night. He didn't like to be one of the crowd. Besides, he figured, beautiful women are always much more interested in the guys who ignore them.

But at about two a.m., with almost everyone gone, he started talking to her.

"Have a good time?"

"Yeah," she said. "It was fun. I wanted to get away from my work and do some dancing."

"What are you working on?"

"I'm in this play at the Drama Shop."

"Oh yeah? That's great. Much of a part?"

"It's pretty big. I play a kind of screwy, rebellious teenager." She seemed excited.

"Sounds just like you," he said.

"You should come see it."

"Definitely. I almost never go to plays. It would be interesting. When's it opening?"

"Who knows? They're talking about five or six weeks from now, but it seems like there's so much to do."

"I'm writing a play," he said.

"Really? That's wonderful. I didn't know you were into that."

"It's the first one for me, kid," he said. "I don't know if it's any good. But I got one act finished."

"I'd love to see it," she said.

"You know, that might be a big help. I don't know anything about the theater. I'm just going on instinct. Maybe you could point me in the right direction."

"Sure. I'd love it. I'll come by sometime, okay?"

"That would be terrific."

Willie had been to only a few plays in his life. When he was eighteen, he saw Albert Finney in *Luther*. He was a freshman in college and got a job with the Post Office as a Christmas assistant, working the graveyard shift at Gracie Station. One night he decided to report to work late so he could catch a play. He loved *Luther*. He was so far from the stage, he could hardly see the actors. But from what he could tell, Finney was beautiful.

He also saw *The Royal Hunt of the Sun, Hair* (because his salesman brother-in-law had bought tickets for a client who couldn't use them), *The Subject Was Roses,* and a few college musicals, and stuff by Beckett, Pinter, and Behan.

But the theater remained an alien world to him. He could never remember the right procedure for getting tickets. Actors and actresses always seemed a little phony to him, too hooked on being Up and Vibrant, like people in gay bars. Movies were much simpler.

Willie was a lower-class snob. His play was designed to make him rich and famous. He knew it was terrible. But maybe Janet would come by with some advice. And maybe one thing would lead to another. And who knows what could happen?

*   *   *

Willie longed for the days of Richard Nixon. He wished Nixon would make a miraculous comeback. He hated Nixon, just like all his friends. In the old days, Willie had marched against the war, beaten the draft, written for underground newspapers, demonstrated for civil rights, played for Viet Cong birthday parties, and Marched on Washington. But now he lived in Washington. And Richard Nixon, and the great saga of his collapsing presidency, had been the most entertaining spectacle in town.

Nixon on color TV, dripping with sweat, his face

drooping, his eyes shifting. A press conference or a speech. And everything he uttered—every sentence, every word—a lie. A completely conspicuous lie. A polygraph machine as big as the Ritz could not absorb the lies and distortions that poured out of Nixon's mouth. Willie loved it. It was crazy. This maniac was the President! And he was a born liar. He was incapable of telling the truth. His eyes darted around furtively, he stammered, he cleared his throat. Nixon was a classic. Any moron could see he was full of it.

But now they had taken Nixon away. No more shady attempts to weasel out of the tangle of lies strangulating his administration. No more of those wonderfully embarrassing, self-conscious statements in which Nixon would refer to himself in the third person as "The President." A one-man gong show, better than a chorus line of LBJ's showing off their surgery scars. But now he languished in Napoleonic exile in San Clemente, all that awkward wickedness gone to waste. If others invented the banality of evil, Nixon gave the world the clumsiness of evil.

For Willie, Washington was not the same with Nixon gone. He had always been of two minds about Washington. He loved the clean, tree-lined streets, the beautiful houses and apartment buildings, the efficient, civilized atmosphere of the city. His living room window gave him a terrific view—a row of pretty houses in different colors. In the winter, with snow on the roofs, he pretended he was in Switzerland. In New York, he had developed a rampant paranoia. He hated taking the subway from Manhattan to the Bronx. That meant a ride through Harlem. At 125th Street, he always expected a gang of young blacks to invade the train and start slicing people up. New York had given him fear—of the streets, of subways, of Puerto Ricans, of blacks, of going out or staying in, of everything. He loved New York. But along with passion came fear. Washington wasn't as scary. He was comfortable in D.C.

But it also bored him. The big government buildings decorated the city like giant tombstones. The department of this or that. Endless offices, countless bureaucrats. Far too many lawyers. Men in suits. And thousands of frail old ladies, remnants of the corps of Southern belles who came to Washington to work for Roosevelt and The New Deal. And all the blacks. They came to escape the poverty and segregation of the South. A lot of them hit D.C. and stayed put. Even before the 1954 Supreme Court ruling on segregation, the whites started moving out of the nation's capital to places like Arlington, Alexandria, and Bethesda. Willie felt like he was in South Africa. The blacks were in another world. And they were eighty percent of the city's population. That left twenty percent white. And most of them were in an even more alien world. Where were all the Irishmen, Italians, the IRT trackmen, the garbagemen?

Garbage. He couldn't figure out about the garbage. In New York, you couldn't miss it. It was piled up on the sidewalks in dilapidated cans and old brown burlap bags. When New York had a garbage strike, the joke was, "how can you tell?"

Washington had no garbage. No cans on the sidewalk. No garbage trucks blocking traffic. No crash of cans as the garbagemen carelessly threw them back to the sidewalk after dumping them out. He knew a guy who got a summer job as a garbageman in the Bronx and lost one of his legs kicking the garbage into the steel mouth in back of the truck. The mouth took one of the guy's legs along with the garbage.

There were no pizza parlors or candy stores either. Willie had lived on pizza for about eight years. And no stores like Bobkoff's on Fordham Road where you could get anything you needed from underwear and shoelaces to sleeping bags. He still bought most of his clothes on trips to New York.

Janet was from Washington. Or the suburbs of Washington, where most white people who are from Washington are really from. He tried to remember exactly what she looked like. All-American. Definitely. Not very tall, but no shrimp either. Those gigantic eyes. A smile that seemed always on call, ready to dazzle its beholders with a flash of perfect teeth. Brown hair. Flawless features. Freckles that seemed wholesome, like the bubbles in Coke. She could hold her own among the faces and figures in the Sunday *Times* Fashion Report. Like those fashion models, her beauty seemed to lack the promise of passion. But that unattainable quality became part of her appeal.

After the night of the party at his apartment, Willie hoped Janet would contact him. He decided he wanted her badly. There were lots of things Willie wanted badly: money, success, fame, immortality. He wanted good health and good looks, nice clothes, delicious meals, intimate friendships, respect, unforgettable sex, exotic vacations. But when his desires became centered on another person, it meant that that person represented everything he wanted badly.

Willie realized this was not a good position to put someone in. Still, when it came to love, Willie lost his head. Love blew everything else away. Independence, promiscuity, solitude, freedom—all the things he saluted in life—crumbled to nothing when love struck him. Nothing else seemed important. Willie was an intelligent man. He knew love was stupid. When he made mistakes, he knew what they were and why they happened. But he didn't care. He gave himself over to love, to the life of the emotions. Forget being sane and rational. How could anyone be sane and rational and in love at the same time? You had to choose.

He was certainly not in love with Janet. After the party, he found himself thinking about her more, gathering a sense of his attraction to her. He didn't want to fall in love with her. He had had enough crazy romance in his life.

She was too beautiful. He would never be able to hold on to her. Men couldn't resist her. They were all over her all the time. Willie couldn't deal with that. The jealousy would drive him up the walls.

On the other hand, he might be all wrong. She might fall in love with him and become a real drag. A clinger. He had been on both sides of the love situation. He knew it could be worse to have someone in love with you than to be yourself hopelessly in love with another.

One day, a week and a half after the party, Willie heard someone shouting up to his window. It was Janet. He threw the key down to her and she came up.

"I hope it's okay to stop by without calling," she said. "Remember you told me to come by and read your play?"

"Hey, don't apologize," Willie said. "It's great to see you."

That was how they started. Willie knew he should be wary: she can have just about any man she wants, so I'd better be careful. Don't fall in love with her, he told himself.

They spent the afternoon together. Janet said she liked his play. He liked Janet. When she was about to leave, he took her in his arms by the door and kissed her.

"Is this all right to do?" he asked. She looked confused. Or puzzled.

"Yeah. I guess."

"I guess men come on to you a lot," Willie said. She laughed with resignation.

"God. All the time. Sometimes it can really drive me crazy."

"Well, look, I really like you. I mean, I won't give you any trouble."

"You're not giving me trouble," she said. "I didn't mean to lump you with all other men."

"That's good," he said. "Do you want to get together again? I really had a good time being with you."

"Yes. I want to see you again."

"Let's go to a movie," he said.
"You're on."

Then Willie started thinking about her more and more.
That time at Christopher's seemed like ancient history. He
was glad he was too messed up back then to be interested
in her because he figured she must have been impressed
with him. There weren't too many men around cool
enough to wind up in bed with Janet Ross and not make a
move. He felt more and more attracted to her.

They made a date to meet in front of the Cerberus in
Georgetown. When Willie got there, he couldn't spot
Janet at first because of all the people milling around the
theater. Then he saw her. She was leaning up against a
parked car smoking a Vantage. She looked great. She was
wearing a tight blue tank top and blue jeans.

She had that distant, magnetic, ex-acid-freak look on
her face, in her eyes, that protected her from the world. She
distanced herself from the people around her, but not in a
snobby way. It was almost religious.

Willie knew he was starting to fall. Those eyes, the
freckles, her shapely breasts under the tank top, her All-
American look. The smile of the century. And plus, he
thought, she's intelligent and talented.

The show was sold out. Willie suggested they go back to
his place and watch some tube instead. He didn't want to
think about sex. Never count on sex, he thought. Just hope
for it. He wasn't pushy about sex. Don't put on any pressure. Just let it happen if it's going to happen.

The TV was in the bedroom, his air-conditioned sanc-
tum. They got high. Willie cooked up two grilled cheese
de luxe, with ham, tomato, and onion, and they retired to
the bedroom. There was nothing but junk on the television. They sat up in the bed, against the headboard, and
ate their sandwiches. When they finished eating, Willie

pulled a joint out of his cigarette pack.

"This was supposed to be for the movie," he said. "Maybe it will make the TV seem better."

"I wish they'd show more good movies on television," Janet said.

Willie kept switching the channels, hoping to stumble on something good. They talked and smoked cigarettes and gave only a small margin of attention to the tube.

But the TV helped. It was like having an insane, shrieking madman in the room with them. A third partner, a crazy person you just ignored. But Willie didn't want to turn it off. It provided protection, a technological blessing. With the robot of American consciousness right there in the bedroom with them—blinking, selling used cars, killing people, trying to make you laugh, seducing the minds of an entire generation with its magnetic glow in dark rooms all over the country—how could their situation be anything but wholesome?

She leaned across his lap to put out her cigarette. He loved it that she smoked. She gave her body a lot of attention—ate the right food, did yoga exercises, frequented a masseuse. Smoking seemed like something she would abhor. But, no, she loved to suck all that Vantage smoke into her lungs and blow it out her mouth in white clouds as sensuous and elusive as she herself seemed to Willie. She told him once she thought of cigarettes as a trusted friend, like someone who'd always be there when you needed him.

When she leaned over him, he put his hand on her and gently pushed her down so that she was lying across his outstretched legs. He started touching her. She didn't say anything.

"This okay?" he asked.

"Yes," she said. Her voice was barely audible. Willie kept going.

"Christopher told me you were involved with someone."
"Oh, yeah? What does he know?" Willie asked.
"It's not true?"
"I don't know what's true."
"You're being evasive."
"No questions, okay? Let's pretend this is *Last Tango*."
"Okay with me," she said.
"Like I told you before, I'm interested in you. And Maria Schneider. Maria Schneider is your only competition."

Sometimes Willie couldn't sleep at night because of fear. He was terrified. Lying in bed, stoned, alone in his dark room, suddenly a sense of mortality would come over him. It was so real and overpowering. Even though no one was shooting at him, he knew how close the final curtain was. He couldn't keep his legs still. His whole body shook with restless, nervous anxiety.

When he was five, he had his first brush with death. He was with his best friend, Brian O'Shea. The two little boys went to Willie's apartment with their new waterguns. They filled the guns up in the bathroom and started to leave. Mrs. Flynn, Willie's mother, was ironing in the front room. She called out to the two boys as they were about to run out the door: "Be careful crossing the street! Willie, Brian, do you hear me?"

The boys heard her, but they were gone in a flash, full of excitement. They ran down the stoop of Willie's building, squirting their guns in the air and whooping it up like the cowboys in the movies.

Willie took off across the street, with Brian ten feet behind him. Daly Avenue was a little Bronx side street off Tremont Avenue, the main drag. In those days the neighborhood was working-class Irish. Most of the adults, including Willie's and Brian's parents, were immigrants.

There were a few little houses at the other end of the block. And across the street stood the Catholic grammar school where Willie's father worked. But the rest of the buildings were tenement houses. Brian lived in the building next to Willie's.

When Willie reached the curb of the sidewalk in front of the school, he knew something had happened. Whenever he remembered that day, it was like a silent movie. When he turned around to see what had happened, in his head there wasn't a sound to accompany the scene that lay before him. Just an eerie, dumb silence.

His friend was dead. The truck had knocked him back across the street. Willie stared in shock at his friend. Brian sat propped up against the tire of a car parked in front of Willie's building. His forehead was gone. There was just a red hole between his eyebrows and the top of his head. Vomit poured out of Brian's mouth all over his shirt.

Willie didn't know how long he stood there next to the truck staring at his friend. He didn't remember when they took him away. And he never heard a sound.

He saw Mrs. O'Shea run out of her building to the scene of the accident. When she saw Brian, she screamed and fainted. Mr. O'Shea picked her up in his arms and carried her back inside. Someone wrapped Brian in a coarse army blanket.

Brain's wake shocked Willie. His friend's forehead had miraculously reappeared. Willie didn't understand this at all. But this new concept, death, mystified him even more. They told him Brian had gone to Heaven. But, wait a minute, Brian lay right there in this fancy box, surrounded by flowers, dressed in his First Communion suit. Why didn't he just wake up?

Willie could never again stand the smell of flowers. That smell went up his nose, into his imagination, and chilled him inside.

Brian's death turned out to be only the introduction. Right from the age of five, Willie felt like he was getting beaten over the head with human mortality. Now he was twenty-nine and starting to calm down a little. But it hadn't been easy. For one long stretch he found himself seriously twisted up inside. It started when he was twenty-six and lasted for about a year and a half.

He had to stop smoking pot. Every time he smoked, he went crazy. He couldn't swallow without difficulty. He couldn't walk down the street without an overwhelming sense of doom. He would be murdered, or maimed for life, or a safe would fall on him, or a big Mack truck would run him over. He used to love cold weather, but during his big fear of those days, he shivered and his teeth chattered whenever the slightest chill in the air hit him. Dope made it worse, so he just stopped.

Sometimes he was afraid to leave his apartment. Nothing seemed safe. He knew he was going crazy, but it seemed very real to him. He had had too many close shaves. And he'd seen Brian O'Shea and some of his other friends, and his mother, and his father, and uncles and aunts all disappear into the void of his blackest memories. Maybe if he never went out, he could escape their fate.

Christopher Early talked Willie out of his seclusion with promises, dreams, and ambitions. Christopher was a great talker with that special Celtic gift for making his life the focus of a fabulous narrative with a happy ending. He wanted Willie to be part of the story. And Willie was getting so bored with his fears that he was happy to sign up for Christopher's happiness plan.

But Christopher liked to get credit. In his more insecure moods, he was capable of believing he was the cause and everyone around him the effect. He turned Willie on to books, movies, records, to things Willie hadn't known about before. But forever after, he couldn't help reminding

Willie, "Hey, don't forget, I turned you on to that." This annoyed Willie, because he turned Christopher on to a few things himself.

But when Willie woke up with Janet the morning after they first made love, he silently thanked his absent friend. If it weren't for Christopher, Willie might never have met Janet. But now here he was, feeling good for the first time in ages.

Willie offered to make Janet a poached egg for breakfast. He ate the same thing every day: a poached egg in the morning, a grilled cheese sandwich for lunch, a hamburger (usually at the Childe Harold) for dinner. He could cook any kind of breakfast—omelets, French toast, pancakes. But he usually ate a poached egg. It was easier on his nervous stomach.

Janet turned him down. "No thanks," she said, "I never eat breakfast."

"It's the most important meal," Willie said.

"You go ahead," she said. "I'm going to do some yoga."

"You do yoga?"

"Yeah."

Willie fixed himself an egg, ate it quickly, and went into the living room. He started to get turned on again. Janet was lying on the rug in the middle of the room, breathing deeply.

"What are you doing?" Willie asked.

"Deep breathing."

"Well, be careful," Willie was suspicious of yoga, running, aerobics, weight lifting, calisthenics, mountain climbing, of anything that seemed physically exerting. He was of the opinion that if your body is working reasonably well, you should leave it alone.

"This is good for you," Janet said. "You should try it."

"No thanks," Willie said. "I'd probably have an asthma attack."

"This would probably prevent asthma."

"Listen, there's a lot of good Americans out there making Tedrals and Isuprel inhalers and other terrific drugs for asthma. You want to see all those decent people out of work?"

"You're silly. I bet if you learned to stand on your head, you'd get rid of a lot of problems."

"That's okay—I have enough problems right now just standing on my feet."

"I'm serious," Janet said.

"Why, what does it do?"

"It takes the pressure off your internal organs and helps your circulation."

"Show me," Willie said.

He watched as she slowly lifted her legs off the floor till her body was upside down. She looked magnificent, he thought. What a specimen.

"See, it's easy," she said, a voice breaking through her body's concentration.

"Yeah, for you," Willie said.

"C'mon, you can do it. I'll show you."

"Never. Not a chance."

She looked disappointed. She lowered her legs and stood up. She shrugged, as if to say "Who cares? Have it your own way."

Willie knew he had made a mistake. He should have given it a try. But he didn't think she would take his refusal too seriously.

"I got to get going," Janet said.

"You sure you don't want any breakfast?"

"Yeah. I have a million things to do."

"What are you up to?"

"I have to find a new apartment soon. And I have to go over to the Drama Shop. Just errands."

"Well, look, I thought last night was really nice. I mean, I had a good time."

"So did I."

"So, let's keep in touch."

"We will," she said.

He embraced her and kissed her before she left. But she seemed like she had already gone.

He went back into the kitchen and washed his breakfast dishes. Willie had an obsessive need to clean up after himself immediately, or as soon as possible. He had a one-bedroom apartment in the cheapest building in Dupont Circle. It was an old building with antique plumbing and wiring that Willie figured must have been installed by Thomas Edison. In the summer, with dozens of air-conditioners fighting the semi-tropical D.C. weather, the building's electrical system broke down frequently. But Willie didn't mind. His place reminded him of the Bronx. At $160 a month in rent, he could just about afford to live well if his band picked up enough jobs and he sold plenty of pot. Once in a while, he made a few bucks writing reviews for the local papers.

He kept his apartment as uncluttered as possible. No couch, no big easy chairs. What furniture he had, he picked up for next to nothing at thrift stores—two old rocking chairs, three mirrors, two desks, four bookcases, some other stuff. On the walls of every room, including the bathroom, he hung photographs and paintings. The photographs were pictures from his past (there was one of Willie with his mother and Brian O'Shea, taken at Rockaway twenty-five years ago) or of his friends. There were two photographs of Christopher Early, who loved to have his picture taken. In one of them, Christopher looked like a handsome leading man from a thirties movie. In the other, Christopher's hair was long and wispy and streaked with gray. He could pass for an old Irish tinker woman. Christopher's complex personality was mirrored in the two photos. He could seem like a tough young Irish punk one minute, and the next like a delicate, slightly feminine artist on the threshold of middle age. Ever since Christopher moved to New York, Willie found himself talking to the photographs of his friend.

Jack Harte kept promising to give Willie a photograph, but Jack was never too reliable about such promises. Willie did have a little picture of him and Jack taken in one of those 4-for-25¢ machines they used to have at Union Station. Willie stuck the picture in the corner of his bedroom mirror. Jack in his wool hat stared out at the world with a wise, tough look in his eyes. His thick mustache emphasized his old-world appearance. Willie, with his short hair and sunglasses, looked like a C.I.A. agent.

He would have to get a picture of Janet. He already missed her. I blew the yoga business pretty bad, he thought. I should have stood on my head, show her I'm open, willing to change. Willie had his habits, his routines. They were a way of dealing with chaos, although they made him seem inflexible to others. Some of his friends thought he had attitudes that usually come with old age. Willie had a quotation from Flannery O'Connor on his bulletin board: "Routine is a condition of survival."

"You gotta do something to keep back the Void," Willie told Jack. "Man, I'd be slobbering around in the grip of fear and craziness if I didn't put some structure on it." Jack understood.

Willie got dressed and packed up his instruments. His ride was due in about forty minutes. They had a job in the country, somewhere in Virginia. A picnic to raise money for women candidates. Lorne Green would be there.

He could smell Janet everywhere. Willie had an acute sense of smell. "Nose like a bloodhound," he told people. He stuck his nose in the pillow Janet had used all night. Soap, Vantage smoke, sex odors. But you couldn't break the smell down. Everybody had a distinct smell. Willie now had Janet's registered forever in his mind. In the living room, he looked at the place on the floor where she had stood on her head. I have to get a picture of that girl, he thought.

Willie went downstairs to wait in front of the building for his ride. A beautiful spring day, near the end of May. D.C. at its prettiest. Willie felt a sense of relief. Janet. Maybe she would be the answer to his problems, to the things that troubled him inside. Love scared him, sex confused him, but he was ready to accept help. He was bored with himself. Janet Ross. He really liked her. She could be remote, hard to get at. You can't judge anything after only one time with someone, he thought. And underneath the success of their first night together, he still sensed that lack of passion, as opposed to his rabid devotion to physical pleasure. But he thought, well, maybe I can tone it down, not be too threatening, too demanding. And maybe if I do, she'll really come alive and start to crave it. He would be cool. Solid. Together. Different from other men. She would be turned on by that and fall in love with him.

Joe, the bass player, pulled up in his big station wagon. Willie put his instruments in the back and hopped in up front next to Joe. Joe lit up a joint and passed it to Willie. This is fine, Willie thought. Lovely spring day, about to get stoned out of my mind, beautiful new lady in my life, good music from WHFS on Joe's radio. Life isn't so bad. Look at all those people in jail. Or the handicapped. Or the starving masses in India. When he was a little boy, Willie always said a "Hail Mary" to himself every time he saw a cripple on the street.

"How's it going?" Joe asked.

"Very nice. No complaints," Willie said.

"Ready to knock them out?"

"Turn me loose," Willie said.

Willie loved meeting famous people. Lorne Green, star

of "Bonanza" and numerous Alpo dog food commercials, roamed around the picnic in all his glory. He seemed short and fat to Willie. He dressed more like a lawyer than a cowboy, but his face had that rugged Bonanza look. What struck Willie most was Lorne Green's body. He seemed to be made out of cardboard. There was no back to him, just front. A lot of face and gut with nothing to back it all up. Willie wondered if Janet would be impressed that he mingled with Lorne Green. It would be something to talk about.

The band finished the set and Lorne Green strode towards the stage to make his speech. "You guys are great!" he said to the boys in the band.

Willie rehearsed what he would say next time he saw Janet: "Hey, guess what? Lorne Green thought we were great."

Willie didn't hear from Janet for over a week. During that week he became nervous. She's probably got six other boyfriends I don't know about, he thought. Makes sense. She's beautiful, mysterious. Then he remembered her aloofness, the way she seemed to remove herself from any threat of physical or emotional passion. No, this ain't the kind of girl who thrives on a heavy diet of sex and male attention. She picked me out of all the men chasing after her. So, I better do something about it.

He called her day and night for a few days, but she didn't answer. Finally he got lucky. She answered the phone.

"Miss Ross? You probably don't remember me," he said. "We met at the Meat Eaters' Ball at the Hilton in 1968— remember? I told you about my idea for mentholated potato chips."

Janet laughed. "Look, mister," she said, "why don't you stop making these ridiculous calls. It's driving me crazy."

"Seriously, how've you been?" Willie said.

"God, I've been frantic. Rehearsals every night. And I started selling jewelry again on the streets."

"Where? Connecticut and K?"

"Yeah."

"Getting rich?"

"No, getting hassled a lot. But I had to do something. I'm just about out of money."

"Well, listen, I just got a cashier's check for a million dollars, tax free. So I can afford to treat you to dinner, if you're interested.

"I think I'd be interested."

"How about tomorrow night at the Childe Harold? Best hamburgers in town," he said.

"I can't tomorrow," Janet said. "Maybe tonight, though. How's tonight for you?"

"I think I can squeeze it in." Willie had no other plans.

They sat in the back of the restaurant. The dimly-lit interior and brick walls made the place seem like a cave. Or the catacombs. The bartender kept the jukebox volume jacked up loud. The jukebox ranked among the best in D.C., in Willie's opinion. Everything from Dylan, to Hank Williams, the Rolling Stones, Van Morrison, and Willie Nelson.

Janet seemed spaced out again, untalkative. They ordered drinks. Janet wanted a Tequila Sunrise. Willie ordered a rum and coke. Willie loved to talk. The Irish called it "crack." "Great crack" from an Irish musician could refer to either the talk or the music. When you got deep into either, Willie believed, there's not much difference.

But when Willie found himself faced with a silent partner, he always started to babble. With another talker, he talked, relaxing into the rhythms of conversation, the sensuous flow of voices. And like most good talkers, he loved to shut up and listen whenever someone else ran off with all the right words.

But around all those shy non-talkers, Willie panicked.

He got nervous, self-conscious. He'd start to blurt out anything and everything that came to mind. He told dumb jokes or talked about his health, his cat, his past, his diet, insignificant events of his day, his close shaves, his schemes, any gossip he'd heard, newspaper articles he read, TV shows or movies he saw. He even talked about the weather.

Willie tried to control it. After a night of desperate, non-stop monologues delivered to quieter members of the human race, he always felt guilty. He meant for his talk to stimulate theirs. But usually it made them retreat more into their silence, bewildered and intimidated by his performance.

He knew Janet could talk if she felt like it. But tonight she clammed up. Willie took this as a form of rejection. But he didn't want to fall into his nervous babbling. When the drinks arrived, they sat there sipping together in silence. Willie tried not to stare at her. That was difficult. Everyone stared at Janet. Such magnetism, he thought. Sam Cooke on the jukebox sang "You Send Me." Willie lit up a cigarette. He had to say something.

"You like Sam Cooke?"

"What?" Janet said.

"DO YOU LIKE SAM COOKE?"

"Sam Cooke?" she repeated, still not sure what he was talking about.

"Yeah. That's who's singing."

"Yeah, I like it," she said.

"This is the best jukebox in town," Willie said.

"What?"

"THIS IS THE BEST JUKEBOX IN TOWN!" Willie felt like he was screaming. Other patrons looked at him disdainfully.

"It's a little loud," Janet said.

They went back to his apartment after the burgers, Willie checked the movie guide in the paper.

"Hey, do you want to see this Margaux Hemingway thing tonight? Supposed to be lots of sex and violence."

"Where's it playing?" Janet asked.

"Down the block. Loew's Embassy." He pronounced it Low-ees."

"Lows," Janet corrected him, "as in the opposite of highs."

"That depends," Willie said. "In the Bronx it's Lowees. As in, this day thou shalt be with me in the Lowee's Paradise. And it's cock-a-roach, hal-a-vah, and birtday."

Willie wore his white painter's pants and a tee shirt. Janet had on a baggy pair of '30s-style men's pants and a white blouse. She always seemed very fashionable to him. He watched her as she glanced through the movie guide. That night with her last week seemed distant to him now. All kinds of worries started erupting in his mind. Maybe that night was it. The beginning of the end. Maybe she just wants to be friends.

Willie thrived on worry. He looked for things to worry about. He worried about money, death, and sex. He worried about his hair and his chances for success and fame. He worried about getting wrinkles, about tobacco stains on his teeth, about characters in books or movies. He worried about crime, America, and nuclear war.

"They now have the potential to wipe out the entire human race," Jack told him one night in Kramer's.

"Wait a minute. That's not true," Willie said. "If there was a nuclear war, there'd be something like a hundred million survivors in America."

"You're wrong," Jack said. "They can destroy every living thing on the planet. I mean, they don't even know what the multiple effects would be. And the radiation would get what the bombs miss."

Sometimes Jack shot from the hip and Willie made subtractions from his friend's pronouncements. But most of the time Jack spoke with such authority and poise that Willie swallowed it all without question. Jack can be more infallible than the Pope, he told people. Now he had Willie really worried about nuclear war and complete annihilation. And Willie had wanted only to relax, drink his coffee, and chit-chat.

Willie looked for an out. "Maybe it's an easier way to go," he said to Jack. "Everybody goes out all at once. Happy New Year. Instead of all those lonely, personal goodbyes forever."

Jack wouldn't buy it. "No good," he said. "If you die by yourself, you're still alive among the people who knew you and remember you. That's real important to me. I mean, I don't care about personal immortality. But I like the idea of staying alive inside your friends. But if we all die at once, that's it. There's nobody left to remember."

Willie not only worried about Jack, he worried *for* him. In fact, Willie's most perfected form of worrying was his ability to worry vicariously. Jack's only foot-wear, a beat-up pair of sneakers, had holes in the soles. Willie worried that Jack would catch a cold. Jack, however, remained indifferent to his health and never got sick. Willie got sick all the time. Jack wouldn't pay his rent or his phone bill and Willie worried that the Immigration people would send his friend back to Ireland. "That's life," Jack would say.

Janet decided she did want to see the Margaux Hemingway movie. Willie thought to himself, it's crazy to worry about this stuff. Of course she wants to be lovers.

He put his arms around her and kissed her. He hugged her close, pushing her into him, hoping to spark some electricity between them.

"Let's lie down," he said. Janet was squirming.

"Not now," she said. "The movie starts in twenty minutes."

The Age of Transition

*

For the next few weeks, until well into June, Janet had rehearsals almost every night for her part in "Motel Orphans," the Drama Shop's next play. And Willie kept busy playing music. In the space of two weeks, Willie met both Teddy Kennedy and Gene McCarthy. Kennedy showed up at a wedding reception for an ex-Senator at which Willie's band played. McCarthy arrived late at another job they played—a party for a rich liberal couple in the garden of a mansion on Capitol Hill, owned by an even richer liberal philanthropist.

Willie thought Teddy Kennedy should be president. Teddy had the style of his brothers: robust, warmhearted, ready to fight. Teddy had the common touch—he joked around with Willie and the rest of the guys and even sang a song with them. And he was Irish, and Catholic. What more could America ask for?

Willie remembered seeing Jack Kennedy ride by in a limousine during the Columbus Day Parade in New York. October, 1962. Willie played bass drum for his high school band. They never would have shot him in New York, Willie thought. He hated Dallas.

During the Great Debates, they moved the TV into the bedroom where Willie's mother lay dying. His father borrowed a hospital bed from someone, so it would be easier to take care of her. They put the TV on top of the dresser and the whole family assembled in the room to watch Kennedy and Nixon slug it out.

In 1968, Willie worked for Gene McCarthy. He handed out fliers on Fordham Road in the Bronx. He knocked on doors. He wanted McCarthy to be president. McCarthy was not only Irish and Catholic, but a poet as well.

When McCarthy showed up at the party for the rich liberal couple, Willie was impressed. He called Janet the next day.

"Guess what?" he said. "I met Gene McCarthy yesterday. He was at a party I played for." Janet didn't say anything.

"Hello? You still there?" he said.

"Yeah," she said. "So, what happened? You met McCarthy?" She sounded distracted.

"Yeah. He was beautiful. He looks like Jimmy Stewart. We talked about Brendan Behan. He knows his stuff. A very articulate man." Willie heard someone else in the background. Janet said, "I'll be off in a minute" to the voice.

"Someone there?" Willie asked.

"Bob is here," she said. "He's helping me with my lines. The play opens in a week."

"Oh," Willie said. "Well, maybe I should let you go."

"God, I'm going crazy. I have so much to learn."

"Good luck." Willie was upset. It was close to midnight. He was surprised that someone would be with her.

"Is everything okay?" she asked.

"Sure."

"Listen, Bob is just helping me with my lines, y'know?"

"No problem," Willie said.

The next afternoon Janet dropped in on him by surprise. She had been out looking for a job. Selling jewelry on the streets was becoming too much of a drag. The summer heat was unbearable and the men kept trying to pick her up.

Janet rarely dressed conventionally. But because of the job interviews, she wore a dress with a matching jacket and looked like a pretty Capitol Hill secretary. He had never seen her look so straight.

"I like that dress," Willie said. "It turns me on to see you in an outfit like that."

"I hate it," she said. "I feel foolish."

"Yum yum," he said.

"You were upset on the phone last night."

"It's all right."

"Don't worry about Bob. He was just helping me."

"It's cool," Willie said.

"You seem distant."

"I have some bad news."

"What?" she asked.

"I have to go to the hospital next week for some tests on my bladder," Willie said.

"What's wrong?"

"Oh, my doctor seems to think it's strange for anyone to urinate twenty or thirty times a day. He wants to do some tests. Gruesome tests."

"It'll be okay," Janet said.

"I hope so."

"How long will you be in for?"

"Just the day. But I have to have a general anesthetic. So, I'll be pretty out of it."

"I'll come by and take care of you." She sounded very enthusiastic.

"That would be nice," he said. "My brother said he'd pick me up when they're through with me and drive me home. But it would be nice to have you there. I'll be groggy for the rest of the day."

"I'll be there," she said.

"How did the interviews go?"

"Good. I think I wowed them at the Pacifica Foundation."

"I can see why," he said. "Congratulations." She walked towards him.

"Stand up," she said. "I want to put my arms around you."

"Anytime," he said. He held her tight and kissed her.

"I'm falling in love with you," she said.

Willie didn't say anything. They stood in the middle of

the living room. Willie noticed his turntable was spinning. He wondered how long it had been running. Janet pulled back and looked at him, expecting him to say something. He was afraid.

"I'm falling in love with you, too," he said. He hated the way his voice sounded.

▼

CONTROL

MY CAB DRIVER WANTED to attack the Arabs. "We fight like dogs among ourselves," he said, "but when someone starts giving it to us, us Americans know how to get it together."

"Yeah," I said. We were a few blocks from the bar. I told him to drive through this alley off Massachusetts Avenue, a shortcut.

"See, in Vietnam, nobody knew why we were there, so we lost. But everybody can relate to this jive. Hey, I'm forty-five and I'm ready to go over there right now and just take the goddam oil."

When I got to the bar, I took a stool next to Charlie. I told Charlie that America was ready to go to war against the Arabs. Charlie is an energy expert. He was drunk.

"People worried about Skylab," Charlie said. "God, they don't even know what they should be worried about. Forget Skylab. You know, they now have enough in the U.S. arsenal to drop six hundred pounds of TNT on every single person on the planet. That's four billion times six hundred."

"They still use TNT?" I asked.

"Don't be a shmuck, okay? The *equivalent* of six hundred pounds of TNT."

David the bartender was relieved by Michael the bartender.

"What are you drinking?" Michael asked.

"Mist on the rocks," I said.

"How can you drink that stuff?" Charlie said. "It's like syrup."

"Be nice, Charlie," I said. "It's my sweet tooth." Charlie ordered another slow pint.

The band started playing. Pure schlock. Matching outfits. Electric bass, two guitars, and a fiddler who sounded like chalk on a blackboard. After one more set, you could tilt these boys slightly sideways and the Guinness would run out of their ears. Total slobs. They gave the music a bad name. "Wild Rover!" some drunk yelled out.

"Bless us, O Lord," I said.

"What?" Charlie asked.

"Leg of Lamb who takest away the sins of the world, spareribs, O Lord."

"If a bus hit you now, baby, you would definitely go down, not up. Blasphemy opens the doors of Hell."

"Charlie, I envy you."

"I don't blame you."

"I'm serious, man. I'm an anachronism. I can't drive. I'm not handy. I can barely boil water. I just wasn't cut out for the age of technology. And you're an expert on all that stuff. I'm useless. Those monkeys typing *Hamlet* are in better shape than me."

"It doesn't matter, baby," he said. "You think it matters any more whether anyone knows anything? Who cares? Look, all that firepower—the entire U.S. military capability—is controlled by a hundred men. At the most. They can turn us all into hamburger meat. Anytime. And, of course, they're a pack of demented, totally disconnected humanoids. They call the shots."

I shifted myself on the barstool and checked out the band again. The guitar player at the end of the stage kept fooling with the P.A., trying to get a decent balance. Forget it, pal, I thought. The problem's in the music, not the electricity. You could hire Marconi to do your sound and it wouldn't help.

Above the stage hung posters of Yeats, O'Casey, Joyce, Pearse, and Behan, all identified by name at the bottom of each drawing. The management thought they lent the place a touch of class. The walls were sprinkled with other tokens of Celtic culture: mirrors with ads for Glenfiddich, a replica in wood of Dublin's coat of arms, a print of a fiddle.

The place was jammed, as always. Martin the lawyer, completely tanked, stood at the end of the bar slapping people on the back and screaming out drunken incoherencies. Capitol Hill secretaries did ridiculous mockeries of Irish dancing in the tiny space by the front entrance. They jumped up and down as though trying to avoid something on the floor. Four marines sat at a table in front of the band, mindlessly rapping their glasses on the table, totally out of phase with the music. Their insanely short haircuts made them look lobotomized.

People came here to get drunk and make a lot of noise. Far too much noise. Whenever my band plays here, we spend half our time trying to get the audience to quiet down. Towards the end of the night, I have sometimes screamed at them to shut up.

Michael put another Irish Mist in front of me. My fourth.

"So, it's hopeless, Charlie, huh? We don't control anything."

"No. We control one thing."

"What?"

"The family." He drained the glass. "The family," he said again, wiping his mouth with his cuff. "It's the only thing we're in charge of."

"First you got to have one to be in charge of."

"That's right, pal. You're out of luck. Better pick out a nice, fertile young lady and get busy."

"Wait a minute, Charlie. I play music. The generals and the TNT have exactly zero to do with that."

"And they could care less. Wise up. You're just another maggot to them. Squish, you're gone. Go play your little mandolin or whatever it is. You're harmless."

"Hey man, slow down. Music makes the blind see, the lame walk and, you know stuff like that. We're talking about the realm of the miraculous."

Charlie's okay. He has a few drinks and becomes despondent. He knows too much about what's going on in the world and how the system works. And that's very depressing information. It tends to make him gloomy. Plus, he recently broke up with his wife after four kids and twelve years of marriage. His hair's turning gray and right now he's out of work.

I noticed Pinky at the end of the bar. A year ago she was a waitress here. Now she's part of the music scene. She's learning the flute. When I first met her, she was always whispering in my ear, on tip toe, "I'm going to get you yet. You'll see. I want your body." I would laugh. She would laugh. She tries to act saucy. It turns me off. I started dodging her and now she hates me. She doesn't like to be turned down.

Pinky and I stopped saying hello to each other some time back. That's okay with me. I don't trust her. She's always telling people that all the musicians are queer and that there are no more straight men around. Temporary homosexuality strikes many men who find Pinky in pursuit of them. She complains. She bad-mouths everybody. She gets excited by other people's flaws. She stakes out claims on various men and tells her women friends to keep their distance. Once when she whispered that she wanted my body, she finished up by sticking her tongue in my ear. I was taken aback.

I'm not stupid. I figured out long ago that she must be bad-mouthing me too. I didn't come through for her. If she wants my body she'll have to dig it up after I have passed away to my final reward. She knows that. I figure the less I say to her the better.

Michael put yet another Mist in front of me. I was starting to feel very wobbly. I took a little sip then swung around on my stool to face the bandstand. Pinky had moved. She was now sitting on the stool next to mine, with her back to me. I stared at her back. The end of Molly Bloom's soliloquy was embroided in tiny white letters on the back of her vest. All the *yes's* were in red.

Charlie, on the other side of me, was fading. I nudged him with my elbow and motioned with my thumb towards Pinky's back. "Look, Charlie," I said, "Molly Bloom's soliloquy."

Charlie got excited. He squinted in the direction of Pinky's back. "You're right," he said, "it is. That's the most ridiculous thing I've ever seen." Pinky overheard us. She spun around on her stool and looked at me. "Molly Bloom, right?" I said. "I was just pointing it out to my friend here." Charlie bowed his head to her in acknowledgment.

"Charlie, Pinky. Pinky, Charlie," I said.

Now Pinky spoke. "Do you realize that's the first time you've said anything to me in six months?"

"C'mon," I said, "that's not true. We say hello to each other."

"Wrong," she said. "You don't even make eye contact."

"Me?" I said, as though I were one of the few to be spared Original Sin.

Charlie did not like the drift of things. "You two work it out," he said. He left a dollar on the bar for Michael, put his cigarettes in his shirt pocket, and left.

"That's my friend Charlie," I said. "He's an energy expert."

"Who cares?" Pinky said.

"Well, I care. He's a friend of mine."

"Oh, you mean you say hello to him and things like that?"

"What's your problem?" I asked.

"My problem is that you haven't spoken one word to me in six months until tonight."

"I don't think that's true."

"I know it's true," she said.

"You were at the Red Fox two months ago and we talked about fiddle styles," I said.

"I don't remember that."

"It happened," I said.

"I don't care. All I know is you never talk to me. You won't even look at me."

"I'm not aware of anything like that." She smirked at me. I resented her. I don't like her and she doesn't like me. I could see no point to this confrontation.

"It's not just me," she continued. "If it was, I'd think I was neurotic. The fact is a lot of people feel the same way. So I know it's not just me."

The band finished with "The Men Behind the Wire." Then the guitar player said, "Thank you, ladies and gentlemen. We're going to take a short break and be back in twenty minutes. Don't go away." He turned off the stage lights and switched on the juke box.

I finished my mist, put the glass down in front of me, and motioned to Michael to do it again. This was the first drinking I had done in months.

"A lot of people on the scene think you're a total snob," Pinky said. "You walk into Kelly's and don't even say hello to anyone. It means a lot to them. You should say something to them."

"My saying hello to someone doesn't confer any status."

"Yes it does. People care what you think."

"Look, I'm not a snob. Maybe my behavior isn't always easy to understand, but I'm not a snob."

"Don't worry, I understand. You think you're better than everyone else."

"I walk into Kelly's, right? And I look around and say to myself—what should I do, should I go around to every table shaking hands and saying hello like I was running for mayor, or should I just talk to people as I run into them? You know, take it organically. And most of the time, I take it organically. If that looks snobbish to people, I can't help that."

"I'm telling you what people say."

"People are just full of love and brotherhood. I'm tired of apologizing for who I am. People who really know me, they don't have these problems."

"Why don't you come to sessions or parties?" she asked.

"I don't drive."

"Take a cab."

"It's hard getting cabs in this town. I don't like to be stuck anywhere."

I was drunk and starting to feel sorry for myself. I thought everyone loved me. I really thought that. One of the guys in the band walked by us. He recognized me and said hello.

"Nice set," I said.

"Thanks," he said, as he continued making a path through the crowd.

"Liar," Pinky said to me. "They're terrible."

"So, what do you want? You want me to tell them they stink? That's your trip."

"You afraid of the truth?"

"Totally terrified."

I looked up at Behan's picture on the wall. Brendan, watch over me, I prayed. I decided I would finish my drink and leave. There was no reason for me to stick around while this young lady raked me over the coals.

"Pinky, forgive me my sins. I'm leaving."

"You should come to some sessions and learn some new tunes."

"I'll bear your suggestions in mind."

"Sometimes months go by without my hearing your band. When I do hear you, you're still playing the same stuff. you never learn any new tunes."

"Of course I do," I said.

"Name the last five really hot tunes you learned. Or name the last five you even thought about learning."

"Gimme a break."

"You can't name them, right? God, if that was me, I'd have learned about eighteen hot tunes in six months."

"Good for you, Pinky."

"It's a shame," she said. "It really is. You have such a unique style. But you don't care, do you?"

"Lighten up, okay? This music has been important to me all my life."

"It doesn't show. You don't play with any passion."

"Yes I do."

It felt good to be outside. There were no cabs in sight. But I had fifteen minutes to catch the Metro to Dupont Circle before it closed down for the night. I fought the effect of the Irish Mist on my motor control and walked very quickly towards the Metro stop at Union Station.

Pinky upset me. I knew she was right. I hadn't learned any new tunes. I had lots of excuses, but they weren't convincing. But to say I didn't play with any passion— that cut deep. In my mind, I continued the argument. I told her how the music was in my blood, how I played for my mother, God rest her soul, when she was dying.

These were hard times for me. I felt full of fear. I didn't

care how much TNT the generals would drop on me. I was more afraid of my own paranoia. I wanted to control my life and other lives as a way of controlling my fears.

I didn't tell Charlie about the dream I had a couple of weeks ago. In the dream, Charlie appeared to me. He criticized my fussy eating habits and my need for solitude. He accused me of denying life, of being withdrawn, cut off, afraid.

When I woke up, I remembered a direct quote from the dream. "There's a whole cycle of birth and rebirth, death and resurrection. You're cutting yourself out of all of that," Charlie had said. I became indignant in the dream and said, "Don't you think I know about all that stuff?"

I got to the station on time. I sat down on the stone bench and waited for the last train to Dupont Circle. A young woman sat on the other end of the bench. She had a knapsack on the floor between her legs. She got up right after I sat down and asked if I would watch her knapsack "for a second." I said "sure." Then she walked off briskly in the direction of the escalator.

After she was gone a few minutes, I got nervous. What would I do with her knapsack if the train arrived before she returned?

But that particular fear was soon replaced by a much more intense one. I thought, God, what if she's a lunatic terrorist and the knapsack contains a bomb? It all added up: this was the capital of the U.S., the world was crawling with anti-imperialist fanatics, this Metro station was also Union Station and the National Visitors Center. We were only a few blocks from the Capitol building itself. In Belfast, an unattended knapsack would be very suspicious.

Then the woman reappeared and sat back down on the bench.

"Thanks," she said.

"No problem."